A Clowder of Cats

A Joy Forest Cozy Mystery

Blythe Ayne

A Clowder of Cats

A Joy Forest Cozy Mystery

Blythe Ayne

A Clowder of Cats

A Joy Forest Cozy Mystery

Blythe Ayne

Emerson & Tilman, Publishers
129 Pendleton Way #55
Washougal, WA 98671

www.BlytheAyne.com
https://shop.BlytheAyne.com
Blythe@BlytheAyne.com

A Clowder of Cats
ebook ISBN: 978-1-957272-15-3
Paperback ISBN: 978-1-957272-16-0
Hardbound ISBN: 978-1-957272-17-7
Large Print ISBN: 978-1-957272-18-4
Audio ISBN: 978-1-957272-19-1

[**FICTION** / Mystery & Detective / Cozy / General
FICTION / Mystery & Detective / Women Sleuths
FICTION / Mystery & Detective / Cozy / Cats & Dogs]

BIC: FM

DEDICATION:

For cat and mystery lovers everywhere.
Welcome to the year 2032.

Table of Contents

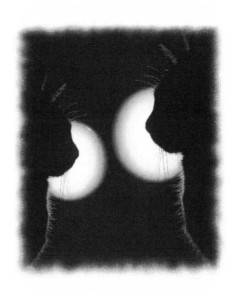

Chapter 1

Security Breach!

A s I triumphantly came to the finish line with my project on Sri Lanka, thinking there was no stopping me now, and for once I'd make a deadline, and my client would be thrilled ... the beautiful 3-D nural net of my project dimmed as my computer interrupted my work.

"There is someone at the front door."

A small hologram of a tall, imposing woman, in layers of flowing dark green, turquoise, and purple silky clothing, stood at my front door. Then she paced in a strange jerky, and at the same time, graceful, motion up and back on my front porch.

"*Who the H-E-double-hockey-sticks is that?!*"

"It's ..." My computer began.

"*I don't care who it is,*" I grumbled.

"But, Dr. Forest, you just asked...."

"I was being rhetorical."

Robbie, my robot cat, curled up at my feet, neither asleep nor awake, jumped up and looked at the woman in the hologram. I heard him scan through his data banks. "*Oh! Wow! It's Evanora Montana!*"

"Who is Evanora Montana? And why are you so excited about her?"

"Me, personally, not so excited. But I'm looking at her biography, and, *hmmm* ... she's pretty colorful."

As I continued to watch the interloper, she came close to the security camera and made a gesture over the lock.

"*Breach of security! Breach of security!*" Computer shrieked.

"Yes!" Robbie yowled. "*Breach of security, breach of security!*"

"*I got it!* Quiet down everyone. *How* did that woman unlock my front door?"

"I was trying to inform you," Robbie said, following close on my heels as I scurried through the house to the front door, "she's a famous *witch*. I'm guessing she used witchcraft on your super-duper security system. And, by the way, as I'm also part of your security system, it feels pretty nasty."

"Hologram," I commanded as I arrived at the front door. I wanted to see if the woman would *dare* to open my door, after already illegally breaching the security system.

She stood, her hand over the door latch, with a look of hesitation. That's when I noticed she had the most astonishing lavender colored eyes.

But another thing threw me for a huge loop ... she seemed inexplicably familiar, although I'd never seen her in my life.

Weird!

"What's she up to, Robbie?" I whispered. "Do you have an impression?"

"She ... she needs to ask you a question. Whatever it is, it's extremely important to her."

"But ... is she crazy? Is she dangerous?"

"*Ahm....*" Robbie hesitated, reading her bios. "No, I don't think so. She's agitated, she's distraught, and it might seem like she's gone a bit around the bend. But she's not going to harm you. She needs something from you."

She put her hands on the door latch, and my alarm system again started to squawk. *"Breach...."*

"Hush," I breathed.

"Do you want me to contact Detective Travis?" Computer asked.

"Not just yet. Let's see what she wants. Maybe she's lost." I didn't believe myself. "But, Computer, if I say 'Travis,' contact Travis."

"Yes, Dr. Forest," Computer replied.

I opened the door. The imposing woman stood even taller than me, which takes some doing. Her flowing, dark jewel-tone garments whirled around her as she stepped through the doorway, even though I'd not invited her in.

She looked down at Robbie with a small frown. "Mechanical," she said with an edge of distaste, as she moved to sit on one of my facing sofas. The swirling fabrics continued to flow about her, and finally the deep sea green, dark turquoise, and shades of evening purple settled. She gestured for me to sit on the sofa across from her. In my own home!

I beg your pardon! I thought. *I'll sit when I'm darn well ready!*

I sat.

"Who are you?" I demanded. "And even more relevant, *how* did you breach my security system?"

She waved her hand—she had impossibly long fingers—as if my question could not be more irrelevant. "Never mind that."

"Are you lost?"

"Please don't bother me with these petty questions." She stared at me without blinking. Absolutely unnerving. Everything about her was unnerving, coupled with the intensity of her lavender eyes.

"I've never seen eyes so intensely lavender in my life," I blurted.

"I prefer to think of them as violet," she replied, continuing to drill through me with her gaze. "I take lippylitherine. It changed the color of my eyes, previously pale brown."

"I've never heard of 'lippylitherine,'"

"No. And why should you? But, listen, I didn't come here to discuss my eye color. I have an urgent issue." She looked again at Robbie. There was no mistaking her disapproval.

Robbie became so uncomfortable that he stole behind the sofa where I sat, out of range of her view.

"Does it have something to do with my robot cat?" I asked, feeling protective of Robbie.

"No. But I do wonder why you have an artificial cat. My reason for coming to see you is about a *real* cat."

"Robbie is very real to me, and I'll thank you to not make disparaging remarks about him. He's emotionally sensitive and neither of us cares to have you invade our home with your negative energy. And again, *how* did you breach my security system?"

"Simple mind over matter. Nothing complicated. Let us get to the point, shall we?"

"Let's. If there is one," I said, wondering *why* I let her in my house.

"Such noisy thoughts!" she said. "I cast a small spell on you."

"*Oh!*" Robbie exclaimed from the floor behind my sofa. "That's why she doesn't like me! She can't cast a spell on me."

"What in the name of Jehoshaphat are you both babbling about? She hasn't cast any spells."

"Indeed!" Evanora declared. "Then how do you explain my disarming your sophisticated security system in but a few moments?"

"I don't," I answered, feeling vexed.

"And you won't, if you refuse to acknowledge the truth. All beside the point!"

"Whatever *that* might be."

"*What. That. Might. Be,*" Evanora-of-the-violet-eyes said in a tone of exasperation, "is, I need you to find my cat."

Shocked, I exclaimed, "I don't find cats!"

"Perhaps you haven't. But the moment has arrived. Even with all my powers, I've not been able to discover where my precious little Booji has disappeared to."

"Again, I don't...."

"I will pay you handsomely, whether you find her or not. Although my pendulum tells me you *will find her.*"

"Well, I'm equally certain that I won't. Because ... *I don't look for cats!* Cats go off for days at a time, don't they? And they come home eventually. I'm sure she'll be back soon." I had no idea what I was saying. I only wished that this strange, stunning, over-bearing woman was out of my house.

Robbie jumped up on the sofa behind me and sat near my right shoulder. I looked over at him, and at the same moment, I heard a peculiar sound from across the room.

Chapter 2
Multiple Personalities

Returning my attention to Evanora Montana, I was shocked to see in the place of the overbearing woman, a little girl, tears pouring from those huge, luminescent, unnerving, violet eyes. "*Booji!*" she cried.

I'm not a monster! I crossed the room and sat beside the little girl, patting her shoulder. Robbie jumped off of the back of the sofa and came to sit on her other side. She reached out her small hand and petted him.

"Oh, Joy," Robbie pled, "you must look for her Booji cat!"

Reluctantly, I nodded. I didn't want to do it, but I couldn't *not* do it. "Are you … are you Evanora?" I asked the little girl as she sat amidst the yards of gem-tone fabrics like the center of a flower.

I saw motion out of the corner of my eye and I turned to see Dickens-the-bio-cat coming around the other sofa. He'd apparently been disturbed enough by all the commotion to wake up, jump down from the bed, and come across the house. I felt a puff of air, and silky blue-green fabric floated across my knees.

I looked back at the little girl, but the adult Evanora had returned. A fascinating aroma of vetiver and berg-amot surrounded us. I moved to the corner of the sofa. Dickens jumped into my lap, giving the intruder a nar-row-eyed study with a small growl.

Dickens almost never growls! I took this as further warning, as if this strange invader was not concerning enough without a growling cat. "Everything about you is disconcerting, and I'm vacillating between agreeing—although I don't know why!—to look for your cat, and telling my computer to call the...."

"Please don't," Evanora begged. "I do apologize that a couple of my personalities have escaped. They are so distraught, as am I, over the absence of our precious Booji. Your bio cat took the little girl away from her grief for a moment. And now I'm back."

"It's all too weird for me...."

"But, Joy…" Robbie said, "It's not about this strange woman, and I agree with you that she is! It's about a cat, Booji, a missing cat. And, if a *witch* cannot find her cat, the cat must be very lost, and may not know how to come home."

Evanora began to make a sort of whining sound. Fearing that she might turn into the crying little girl again, which I truly did not want to see, I shrugged, defeated, giving up the better part of wisdom.

"All right! All right! Let's not get too emotional. I mean, we've already been there. Let's not go there again!"

I petted Dickens and set him on the sofa, then stood. Pacing back and forth between the two sofas with Robbie, Evanora, and Dickens watching me, their heads like metronomes, did not help me concentrate.

I paused. "Let's start with a picture. Please project a picture of the missing Booji."

"Ahhhh, yes, all right." Evanora made a complicated gesture in the air, and the form of a tawny cat materialized. She had markings that I couldn't quite make out, it was as if the picture was out of focus.

"Wow!" Robbie exclaimed.

"What, Robbie?"

"That's a gorgeous cat!" he said.

Meanwhile, Dickens stood up and growled, the fur rose on his back all the way to the end of his tail. I'd never seen such a reaction from him.

"But the picture is out of focus," I said.

Evanora waved her hand. The image disappeared. "Not to worry, dear Joy. Not to worry. You'll know Booji when you see her. You don't need to look at a picture. You don't need to look at a picture," she repeated quietly.

I knew I was being hypnotized—I could feel myself going under. The blues and greens of her flowing garments seemed to fill the room, dreamy and watery. My ordinary consciousness slipped while I struggled to not succumb.

Robbie was saying something to me, but I couldn't make it out. Facing the three of them, I felt more out of body than in. Dickens jumped down from the sofa and scurried to the back of the house. He was not having any more of this weirdness!

Robbie got down from the sofa and stood by me, looking up at me, concern on his features.

Suddenly, a resounding command echoed through my little house, practically rattling the pictures off the walls.

"Clark county police! Open up!"

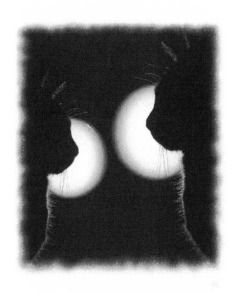

Chapter 3
Not on a Broom

The watery surroundings immediately dissipated, and my familiar three-dimensions returned.

"*Travis!*" I exclaimed, hurrying to open the door.

There stood Travis in all his uniform and glory, brow furrowed. "Are you all right?"

I nodded, then shook my head. "I'm fine. Sort of."

"You had a breach of security."

"Yes. Indeed. I've had a *really strange* breach of security."

He shifted from one foot to the other. "Sorry it took me so long to get here. I waited for you to report. When you didn't, I became alarmed.…"

Evanora stood and floated in all her mystical yards of silky colors to stand by me. "Hi there, gorgeous," she cooed.

I couldn't have been more shocked. I looked from Evanora to Travis. He took a small step back.

"*You!*"

"*Me!* In the flesh!" She said with a small, wry chuckle.

Stating the ridiculously obvious, I said, "You know her?"

"We've met," Travis said.

Evanora chuckled. "Yes," she said with innuendo, "we have met."

"My boss retained her services on a missing person's project."

"Really?" I exclaimed. "But.…" I turned to Evanora.

"I'm too close to my missing little Booji. I can't psychically see her because I'm too traumatized. I *did* try. I have tried and tried. But it's no use. I can't see her."

"Oh!" Travis said with insight. He sighed audibly. "The woo-woo women get together. I'm entirely out of my element."

"We are not 'getting together.' She breached my security system with whatever powers she may have. Frankly, she's kind of scary."

"I can understand what you're saying," Travis nodded. "What do you want me to do about her?"

I looked over at Evanora, and saw a faint shadow of the little girl that had sat on my sofa, crying. "I don't know, Travis. I guess just let us sort this out for the moment." I turned to Evanora. "But I am *not* kidding! You're not to breach my security, disparage my robot cat, or in any other way, upset me, or cause me anything even faintly resembling grief. Do you agree?"

The little girl faded, and Evanora shrugged. "I will do my best, dear Joy, I will do my best. But I'm sometimes difficult to control, even for myself. There's a lot going on in here!" She waved her silky blue, green, purple-covered arms, stirring up a breeze that ruffled my hair and even made the plants on the porch wave about.

"That's a fact!" Travis affirmed, as he turned on his heels and headed for his Space XXX Roadster.

"But even so, Evanora," he called over his shoulder, "do not, I repeat, *do not* give Joy a hard time."

Soon the roadster lifted into the sky and disappeared. I turned my attention to Evanora. Now what? I wondered, through all the tumbling thoughts cascading about in my mind. What sort of a corner had I allowed myself to be painted into? And … Travis knew this peculiar woman, but he'd never mentioned her. And she implied there was something between them.

Ah, well, none of my business, I told myself. None. Of. My. Business.

Right. I glanced over at her, trying to picture her with Travis. That's when I noticed she was quite pretty. I'd been so discombobulated by her invasion and her presence, that I hadn't taken in her facial features, beyond the compelling color of her eyes.

My first impression was that she was "older," whatever that means, but, no. In fact, she was probably about my age.

"Would you be so kind as to take me home?" Evanora asked casually.

Holy-hallelujah-moly! Did this woman have no boundaries, whatsoever? "How did you get here?" I couldn't disguise the incredulity in my voice. A broom seemed logical.

"Not a broom. I walked."

"Do not read my mind! You walked?"

"Yes, I only live a few miles distant. I hoped I might pick up on any recent movement of my precious little Booji. But no luck. I can walk back home, but I thought it might be helpful for you to see where Booji lives."

She was right. If I were to take on this assignment—weird as it was—I should probably know where the cat disappeared from. I nodded, saying into my wrist comp, "Car, come to the front of the house. Evanora, you can get in the car while I get my backpack."

I went to my bedroom. "Okay, you two cats, be good. I'll be back shortly." I expected Robbie to beg to come with me like he always does, but in fact, I couldn't even see him.

Dickens lay sleeping on the bed, in his usual place.

"Robbie! Where are you?"

"Under the bed."

"Are you all right?"

"Ahem, yes—waiting for that scary woman to go away."

"I'm taking her home right now."

"Good!"

"So you don't want to come with us?"

"*Nope!*"

I giggled. "All righty then. You don't know what you might be missing."

"I'm happy to let you tell me."

I went out to the car and climbed in. "Please tell the car your address."

"I don't actually have an address. I'll give the car directions."

"All right. Car, please respond to Evanora's directions."

"Yes, Dr. Forest."

"Take a left out of the driveway," Evanora said. "Go to Main, take a left, and drive for two miles. I'll give you further details at that point."

"Yes, Evanora," the car replied, moving out onto the road.

Soon we were on Main.

Evanora then turned to me and said, "There's nothing between Officer Travis Rusch and me. But, he's so tease-able, I can't resist."

I nodded, without a clue how to respond. I surprised myself, feeling relieved by this bit of info. But I reminded myself: None. Of. My. Business.

I wondered how someone could live within the incorporated city limits and not have an address.

"Car, take a left here," Evanora said. "Go three-tenths of a mile, take a right, take the first left, go one-tenth of a mile, take a left, go three-hundred feet, and there we are!"

The car did as she bid. I looked around in awe. We were in the thick of the forest!

Suddenly, a huge duck flew right in front of us! I shrieked, fearing for his life.

Chapter 4
The Bestiary

The car came to an abrupt halt.

"*Oh! Mr. Quackers,*" Evanora cried, flinging the door open. She started to climb out as the duck came around the door, quacking up a storm in duck lingo.

"Mr. Quackers! What were you thinking?"

The duck carried on his chatter. Evanora nodded.

I became anxious about having the car stopped in the middle of the road. "Either get in or get out. We're in the middle of the road!"

"Oh no, dear, not to worry. I own the road." She waved behind us. "From the last turn we made. No one ever comes down here without my knowing it."

She returned her attention to the duck. "I can't believe you flew in front of the car, Mr. Quackers, that's so dangerous! Don't ever do it again!" She looked over at me. "He thinks he's impervious to any dangers. This isn't the first time. I've had to deal with him when he dances around the coyotes and bobcats, teasing them. But this is a new level of heedless behavior." She picked the duck up and held him close, muttering endearments I couldn't make out, and he replied in kind.

"He's certainly a beautiful bird," I said, noting his fabulous plumage of gunmetal, iridescent green and shades of iridescent brown.

"Hear that Mr. Quackers? Dr. Forest says you're a beautiful bird!" She petted the duck. He cuddled up to her. "Of course, I think he's a beautiful bird. I hatched him myself." Finally, she pulled the car door shut. "Car, please pull into the driveway, here on your left."

The car pulled into the driveway. That's when I took in my surroundings. We passed under a tall, white-but-rusted wrought iron archway covered in vines, with the word "Bestiary" in scrolly, Victorian letters overhead. All around me fluttered and flew chickens and ducks—a windstorm of wings. I saw through the flurry of wings other creatures that I couldn't quite make out.

The car came to a stop before a rickety little house, painted various colors, as if using up odds and ends of cans of paint. Evanora climbed out and put Mr. Quackers down. He scurried off to join his feathered friends and family.

"Come along," Evanora said, moving to the rickety little front door—itself slap-dash painted yellow, pink, deep blue, and a shade of pale green. On the step slept a peacock. He woke and made a raucous call at the sight of Evanora, fanning out his tail, adding a perfusion of colors to the scene.

I slowly climbed out of the car, wondering what sort of wonderland I'd fallen into. "Power down," I said to the car.

"Yes, Dr. Forest."

I made my way across a bumpy, partially graveled driveway, joining Evanora. She opened the door, letting the peacock in before us. "There you go, Rainbow, dear. I've got a treat for you!"

She gestured for me to enter, which I did, with, I must admit, a bit of caution.

It was dark as catacombs, and I dared not take a further step, as I had no idea what I might step upon.

"*Light!*" Evanora declared, coming in behind me. The entire space lit up like a sunny day. I looked around, but saw no source of the light. In fact, there were light fixtures and lamps all about, but not a single one of them was turned on.

"Goodness!" I whispered. Then I remembered. She's a witch.

It took me a few seconds to process what I saw—the complete opposite of the outside of the rickety little cottage. Exotic tapestries hung from the walls, and rich, vibrant, oriental carpets covered the floors. Voluptuous velvet Victorian sofas and wingback chairs complemented the tapestries and carpets, while a warm rose-scented aroma wafted through the air.

Add to the entire mystical environment the fact that surely the interior of the little cottage was bigger than the outside.

The peacock strutted before Evanora as she moved through the house to another room. "Just going to bring a bit of tea for us, dear. Please make yourself comfortable, anywhere. I'll be right back." She disappeared through a jingling beaded curtain in the doorway—depicting a peacock, of course. What else?

"Tea!" I heard her command, followed immediately by the clicking of china and silver. I wondered what her robot was like, as Evanora alone could not possibly instantaneously make so many sounds. "Here's your treat, Rainbow, my lovely," I heard her say, with a call of approval from the peacock.

I looked around the room, contemplating the various arrangements of furniture. I decided upon a sapphire blue wingback chair in front of a wall of ancient books—actual physical books!—their tantalizing spines daring me to pull one of them from the shelf. But I restrained myself, and settled into the chair, studying the tapestry on the wall across from me that repeated the scene on the other side of the wall—a plethora of both familiar and strange creatures.

"Here we are," Evanora exclaimed cheerfully as she came through the beaded curtain holding a tea tray, followed by a tiny woman robot. The robot, maybe all of four feet tall, had a plain but likable face, short, curly, grey hair, a sort of dumpy, plumpy body, and wearing a yellow 1950s house dress, with a pattern of small pink and lavender flowers. Utterly charming!

The little robot brought a small table to where I sat. Then she took the tray from Evanora and placed it on the table. Next, she carried a matching wingback chair, easily a foot taller than she, from across the room, and placed it opposite me on the other side of the little table.

"Thank you kindly, Mrs. Lark. You may rest," Evanora said as she sat. Mrs. Lark moved to the kitchen doorway, then slumped ever so slightly in a state of repose.

"Great name," I said.

"She chose it herself. I gave her about a dozen options, and she chose Lark, without hesitation, from the list. I was pleased, as the lark is just about my favorite bird—after Mr. Quackers and Rainbow, of course." She chuckled. "That is to say, if one can *have* a favorite bird among all the lovable birds."

"I agree."

She gestured to my teacup. "I hope you don't mind trying out my new special blend of tea. I've not had the opportunity to share it with anyone, and I'd love to know your opinion. Please do be honest! If you don't like it, I must know." While she spoke, she fussed with the tea things, pouring the tea into little demitasse china cups with a delicate Victorian scene of trees and river painted on them. She handed me one on its matching saucer, along with a silver demitasse spoon.

"Thank you," I said, slightly overwhelmed. I thought again about the fact that Evanora was a known witch, and I was about to drink one of her concoctions. Angels fear to tread, I thought, as I cautiously took a small sip of the tea.

Holy cannoli! It tasted fabulous! "My goodness, Evanora, it's awesome! I've never had any tea anything like it! What's in it?"

"That is my secret, of course. But I'm certainly glad you like it."

"I more than like it. I'm a tea drinker, but a fussy one. I'm not readily impressed by a new tea, preferring the ones that are tried and true for me."

What were the flavors intermingling on my pallet? I could taste bergamot and cardamom, and a small pinch of ginger. But there remained something else as well, which was beyond me to name. I became aware of an extreme sense of well-being flowing over and through me.

I didn't mind as long as it didn't influence my emotions or sense of reality beyond this lovely glow. This tea was more relaxing than a couple glasses of wine. "Is this glow of well-being I'm feeling part of your intention with the tea?"

Evanora smiled. "Of course, dear Joy, my intention is that it provides the littlest bit of happy glow, and nothing more."

"It's just right at the moment. Perhaps I shouldn't drink any more."

"Oh no, you've felt the full effect in the first sip. It won't increase."

But I wondered if this was true, as the tapestry across the room began to undulate and swell.

Chapter 5

Two Heads are Better than One

I'm sure my eyes must have become as round as the Victorian saucer under my hand, seeing the stationary tapestry begin to move.

Evanora followed my gaze, then giggled. "Oh, that's Heady. Clever creature! She wants to know what's going on in here, as I rarely have company. When she wants attention, she slides open the window that's behind the tapestry, proving that, indeed, two heads are better than one."

Evanora crossed the room to the tapestry. She pushed it aside to reveal an open window through which peered two llama heads.

Attached to one body.

Disconcerting as the sight was at first flush, I couldn't help but be fascinated by this exotic creature.

Evanora looked over her shoulder at me as she petted each of the heads in turn. "This is Heady-Honey," she petted one llama's forehead. "And this is Heady-Sweetie," she added, petting the other.

"Heady-Honey is the extrovert, and Heady-Sweetie is the introvert. She would never think of disturbing me by opening the window, but the other half will have her way! Each is good for the other."

"Is it … is it okay if I come over to her?"

"Of course! That's why Heady opened the window, she wants to meet you."

I crossed the room slowly. All four of the llamas' large, luminous, gentle eyes were on me. I reached out and petted Heady-Honey. "Oh!" I exclaimed, "she's so soft!" I then petted Heady-Sweetie. "And you are too! But … how is it that they … or she, is alive?"

"I'll come out and play with you later," Evanora said. The two-headed creature backed out and wandered off into the yard as Evanora closed the window and pulled the tapestry back over it. "I don't want to have that conversation in front of them, but it is a sweet story." Evanora gestured for me to return to my chair, and she joined me, topping up my tea, then proffering a small dish of lovely sweets. "Turkish delight, Joy, the best in the world. I make it, but this is made by my friend. I have to say he knows how to make it better than anyone, anywhere. Including me."

I took one of the confections and bit into a chunk of heaven. "*OMG!*" I blurted. "I've never tasted anything like this in my life!"

"I know!" Evanora agreed, then she returned to the thread of our conversation. "When the Headys were born on my neighbor's farm," she gestured off to the west, "he happened to come by the next day, and told me a freak event had occurred during the night. He was pretty upset about it. 'Even more frustrating,' he said, 'the monster didn't die in the night like I'd hoped.'

"Of course, every maternal fiber in my being—and I have a lot—was set in motion. Cool as a cucumber, but actually very excited, I asked casually if I can could come by and see the creature. He said sure, but he felt certain she'd probably expired. In any case, he said he hoped it would happen soon, and he preferred it to having to put her down himself.

"When I got to his farm, there were the sweet little Headys, on their four feet, looking as adorable as the day is long. I had to have them! I couldn't imagine putting them down, and I could see that their life force ran strong. So I begged him to let me have the little creature. He said, 'sure, but you'll have to bury it!'

"I felt certain I wouldn't be faced with that. I had to bottle-feed them as I had taken them away from their mother. The vet came and checked them out. He said they were surprisingly healthy. He observed that to all outward appearances, it was only the head and neck that were twins, and the body appeared to be one healthy body.

"I subsequently had Heady fully x-rayed. There are small, residual, entirely non-functional twin organs that do not interfere with her general health.

"When the vet saw the x-rays he said, 'oh those organs are going to cause trouble!' But I ignored him because I knew what would keep the Headys alive."

"And what is that, Evanora?" I asked.

"You know, Joy!"

"I do?"

"Indeed, you do. You, of all people, know better than most what keeps the life force flowing."

I knew what I *thought*, but I didn't know what Evanora thought I knew. Puzzled, I remained silent.

"Just say it!" Evanora said.

"Well, what I would say is love."

"Exactly! Love is the force of life. You see, that's why I've come to you to help me find my precious

Booji. You understand that love is the force behind everything. And even though Booji has decided to go off for a while, you will find her, because you will look for her in a spirit of love.

"So ... tell me what you think of that Turkish delight?"

"It's amazing! Absolutely amazing! I could easily get addicted to it. Please do not tell me where I can get more. An addiction of this sort is something I don't need."

"If you're sure! But I'll have Mrs. Lark wrap you up a few pieces. You wouldn't mind that, would you?" She asked with the slightest of evil grin.

I shook my head. No, I wouldn't mind. "Now then, should we talk about Booji? When did you last see her? What direction is she most likely to have gone? Your property is old growth forest. It seems like it would be nearly impossible to find her if she chose not to be found."

I didn't say what was really on my mind. The sad fact that a cat wandering around in the forest with coyotes and bobcats and bears and even raccoons, would not likely fare well. If her Booji was still alive, it would be nothing short of a miracle.

"She's not been done in by any other creature," Evanora said.

"You *have* to stop reading my mind," I said defensively.

Evanora guffawed. "Well, then, dear, you must learn not to think so loud! Anyway, no, Booji has not been viciously devoured. I can feel her. She's alive. I don't know why she's gone off like this and not come home. She must be so angry with me."

Okay, I'll play along, I thought. "And why would Booji be angry with you? She has a fantastic life here, and you dote on her."

"All true. But we did have a little 'event,' shall I say."

"And what was that?"

Suddenly, my car's siren went off, bleating at top volume. Evanora and I ran out the front door.

Chapter 6
Something to Reflect Upon

W e burst into laughter when we took in the scene before us. Heady-Honey was admiring herself in my car's mirror, but with perhaps a bit more aggression than necessary. Evanora and I walked over to the Headys and the car.

"Dear Heady-Honey," Evanora said, putting her arm around Heady-Honey's neck, "you needn't touch the mirror in order to see yourself, now do you?"

"I was being mauled," the car said with indignation. "The mirror must be cleaned and adjusted," the car continued, while doing just that.

"Good job, Car. I'm sure Heady did not mean to offend you. She was admiring her beautiful self in your reflection. There's nothing to be upset about."

"Yes, Dr. Forest. But should I generally allow llamas to maul my mirrors?"

"If it ever happens again, we'll address it at that time. It seems highly improbable that, other than Heady-Honey, it will ever happen again. But, yes, we'll let Heady-Honey and Heady-Sweetie admire themselves in your mirrors."

"That's very kind of you and Car," Evanora said. "It's interesting to learn that Miss Heady-Honey would feel a need to see herself, given that she has an identical twin that she sees all the time."

"But," I surmised, "that might be precisely the reason for her intrigue. She wants to see her own identity!"

"Good insight, Joy," Evanora said, hugging the Headys. "I'll get you your very own mirror, my dear llama, a big one, and you can look at yourself as much as you please! And your sister can, too!" She led the Headys back into an enclosed corral. "Now be good until I come out to play with you later."

Evanora went back into the house, gesturing for me to follow her.

"So, now, about Booji," I said, looking with a slight bit of longing at the lovely tea and incomparable Turkish delight. "Will you loan me something that belongs to her, one of her toys, or something she is fond of, to help me find her?"

I had the thought that possibly Robbie, being the brilliant robot cat that he was, might be helpful in tracking the missing cat, if we were in possession of something that belonged to her. Despite Evanora's disdain of him.

"Frankly, Booji is not much for toys. But I'm sure I can find something she's been attached to. Let's go see." Evanora led the way through another door I hadn't noticed.

Yet again, the house seemed to expand beyond its external footprint. Four doors surrounded us in a small hall. The first one stood slightly ajar as we passed it. The room inside was dark, and I couldn't make anything out.

"That's Birdie's room," Evanora said.

"Who is Birdie?" I asked, willing to assume it was yet some other sort of exotic creature. I wasn't sure how I felt about seeing it.

"Birdie is my roommate. She … she's not here right now."

The way she said it was fraught with innuendo. As innocently as I could muster, I asked, "Oh? Where is she?"

"I have no idea," Evanora answered in an edgy voice.

Hmmm, I thought, making a mental note—what was that about? And did it have anything to do with Booji's disappearance?

"Here we are," Evanora flung open one of the other doors to a room entirely covered in cat towers, cat condos, and cat houses, from floor to ceiling, with a pathway a human could barely navigate. "This is Booji's room!"

"Holy sweet cannoli, I've never seen anything like it. Why would a cat even consider leaving such a paradise?"

"My feelings, exactly. But my darling Booji has her own ways."

I wandered around in the cat mecca. "All of this for one cat?"

"Yes. Booji is an only child at the moment."

"I see," I said, not at all sure that I did see. "But ... is Booji not chipped?"

"Oh, she's more than chipped. She has eye implants that let me see what she sees and let me know where she is. But she has—and, again, she's quite willful!—she has somehow managed to turn them off, or block them so I can't access them."

I thought again of my dreaded suspicion that Booji was no more, hoping Evanora would not read the thought, as she had been so cavalierly doing. "How would a cat know how to turn off implants? I, myself, would have no idea how to do that."

"She's not a usual cat." Evanora handed me a small blanket. "I've occasionally seen her sleeping on this little blanket. Do you think it will suffice?"

I took the fleecy blanket, covered in a pattern of romping kittens of every description. "Yes. This is perfect!"

"Are you going to try to get a psychic read from it? I've already tried, but, again, Booji is determined, I guess, not to let me know where she is."

"No. Since you ask, I'm going to see if Robbie, my robot cat, that you scorn, can retrieve some DNA and then, perhaps, track her. It's a long shot, I admit."

"Your robot cat might help find Booji? Well then, I adore Robbie. Be sure to convey my apologies for my rudeness to him. I'm not myself. I miss my precious Booji."

Evanora looked as though she might begin to cry, and not wanting that—or anything else that might transpire because of it—to happen, I quickly assured her the best I could. "We will do everything in our power to find the invincible Booji."

Evanora's grey skies turned sunny. "Invincible Booji! Yes, indeed, Invincible Booji. I may even change her name. So perfect, dear Joy! Thank you."

"You're certainly welcome. But ... something continues to nag at me."

"What's that?"

"You seem not to want to tell me, but I do feel I need to ask. Tell me about the 'little trouble' you and Booji had?"

"Oh goodness, I don't think it's a big enough issue to go into...."

"Humor me, Evanora."

"Well, you see, Birdie, my roommate, has this rug that she thinks more of than even living creatures. And well, as it happens, Booji sort of ... that is she, *ahm*, sort of scratched it a little bit. And Birdie went off on Booji. It was quite unpleasant. Because, then *I* got into it, and although I'm not proud of myself, I ended up yelling at both of them.

"I wasn't wrong! Booji should not have scratched Birdie's rug, and Birdie should not have gone off on Booji. I was pretty mad at both of them, and you've seen a little bit about how, when I'm highly emotional, other things about me sometimes happen.

"Stuff whirled around, and Booji took off. Birdie went into her room and slammed the door." Evanora gestured at the door across the hall.

"Everything became quiet. I don't exactly remember what happened then, because I was in quite a state. But the next thing I knew, Booji was gone. And, well, Birdie has been gone since then, too."

"Oh. My. Goodness," I said softly. I could feel the energy of the heightened emotional conflict. I would not have cared to see things flying about, and at that moment, I had more sympathy for Booji and Birdie than Evanora.

"I'm a terrible person. A terrible, terrible person," Evanora whispered. "Birdie has her own life. She goes off on trips from time to time. She generally, of course, tells me where she's going, and when she'll be back. But she hasn't this time. On the one hand, I can't blame her, and on another hand, I can't believe she would add to my anguish. It makes me *so* angry. Plus, of course, it all started because she yelled at Booji. It was not such a big deal. It's just a rug!"

Wanting to see for myself, I stepped across the hall into Birdie's room. *I gasped in shock at what I saw.*

Chapter 7

A Trek to the Himalayas

Evanora stepped into the room behind me. I turned to her, gesturing at the carpet, shaking my head. "First of all, how could one cat do this? Secondly, this is not a small thing! *This is a big deal.*"

Evanora looked down at the carpet as though she had not seen it before. "Oh. *Hmmm,* I guess ... I guess it's a bit worse than I thought. Oh, now, I really am going to cry." Evanora sat down on the carpet, her body began to shudder. "Birdie trekked across the Himalayas and studied with the monks. They *gave* her this carpet. It's *hundreds* of years old. Why did Booji do this?"

I sat on the floor beside her. "That's all in the past now, Evanora. We're in the present, and we must make the best of it. I assume Birdie will come back in her own good time, and you can make it up to her. Although the carpet is damaged, it's possible to have it re-woven, though, no doubt, extremely expensive."

Evanora sighed deeply, as if a huge burden fell off her shoulders. "*It could be re-woven!* I haven't thought of that! Oh, thank you, Joy! I don't care what it costs, I have more money than I know what to do with. My aunt left me everything when she transitioned, and I have a financial advisor who just keeps making millions out of millions. I'll take the carpet to the Himalayas *myself* and have the monks, or whoever makes their carpets, re-weave it, if I have to!"

She leaned over and gave me a huge hug.

The warmth of her happiness flowed right through me. "We're both happier now, right?" I asked.

"*Abso-happy-lutely!*" she exclaimed.

We sat in the happiness-flow for a few moments, until I finally jumped up, inspired to get on with finding Booji. "Let me move on with the project at hand, Evanora."

"Yes, good idea." She patted the wounded carped lovingly and then stood. "I'll have Mrs. Lark pack you a bit of Turkish Delight and a little packet of my tea, if you'd like."

"I'd like it. I'd love it!" I pictured a delightful evening with the two unusual treats.

Soon I was back in the car, after thanking Mrs. Lark, saying good-bye to Rainbow, the Headys, Mr. Quackers, and waving to the general gathering of creatures.

What an experience!

"Okay, Car, let's go home! I have a blanket of Boo-ji's, and I want to see if Robbie can gather some DNA or any other information from it to help me track Evanora's cat. I don't exactly know what I'm doing. It's a long shot."

"That's an excellent approach," the car said, pulling back onto the main road home. "And why don't you have me do the same, get a reading from any of the bios that might be attached to Booji's blanket?"

"You can do that?" I asked, surprised.

"Of course. I maintain the environment in here all the time and part of the process is determining what all the environmental factors are."

"I didn't know that! I mean, I know you keep the environment in here clean and pure and safe, but I've not thought about what all that entailed. How would you take a read of Booji's blanket?"

"Hold it up to my vent."

I held Booji's blanket up to the vent, and the car did whatever was necessary to gather bio information from it.

"Got it!" The car said. "Wow, that's an interesting cat! If we come across her, I'll know it."

"That's good," I said as we pulled into the driveway at home. "Be ready to go. I'll have Robbie give me his opinion about Booji, if he has one after contemplating Booji's blanket, and I guess I'll start driving around looking for her. It's a sure thing that I can't get back into my project with Evanora's energy swirling around me."

"Right, Dr. Forest. I'm ready, as always."

"Hey, Robbie," I called, stepping through the back door. I put my delightful Turkish Delight and mystical tea on the kitchen counter.

Robbie came into the kitchen from the bedroom. "I sense you had quite an adventure at that woman's home."

"I did! I'll give you details later. But right now," I pulled out Booji's blanket, "I need you to give me your take on this blanket that belongs to Booji."

Robbie literally turned up his nose, spun away from me, and sat down on the floor, his tail wagging jerkily in irritation. "I'm not going to do it. That woman is not nice. And I'm not going to do it."

"She *is* nice, Robbie. She has lost her kitty. She's in grief. *You're* the one who said I must help her."

"I felt sorry for the little girl. But the woman is not nice."

"The little girl is part of the woman, and they are both sad. They need us to find Booji."

Robbie continued to sit with his back to me, his tail saying more than words could ever express.

"All right then, I will look for Booji, and you can do your favorite thing. You can stay home and watch Dickens sleep."

"*Awwwrrr*, when you put it that way!" Robbie turned around. "Give me that blanket."

I couldn't help chuckling. Sometimes he was so easy! I knew he loved to go out and about, and really, what could be more exciting for a cat—even a robot cat—than finding a missing cat?

I handed Robbie the blanket. He kneaded and sniffed it, and then kneaded and sniffed it some more. "This is a very interesting cat, I must say—she's kind of big. I'll know her if I see her."

"Given the damage Booji did to Evanora's room-mate's carpet, I'd say, yes, a fairly large cat did that damage. That's good, because I think a larger cat will be easier to find. But let's not say 'if' we see her! Let's stick with 'when.' we see her."

"*When*, of course, when we find Booji. And speaking of when, when do you plan to begin searching for her?"

"This very moment! Are you ready to go?"

"Ready!" Robbie jumped up, flung Booji's blanket around his shoulders, and twirled in a circle, with the blanket swirling out like a cape. "Let's go!"

"Oh, Robbie, you're such a character!" I laughed. "Yes, let's go!" I ran into the bedroom, grabbed up my AR glasses, and threw them in my backpack. Then Robbie and I stepped out to the driveway to the waiting car.

"Oh no, I forgot! We can't go yet!" I exclaimed, hurrying into the garage.

Chapter 8

Into the Forest

"Never mind, Joy, we don't need that," Robbie hollered after me in protest.

"Yes, Robbie, we do." I grabbed the car seat and hurried back to the car. "I'll put it in the front instead of the back, and I'll sit in the driver's seat, instead of the passenger seat, like we usually do. That'll be okay, won't it? You'll be up front with me, be my wingman."

"*Nooooo Joyyyyy!* I'm not a human baby. It's humiliating."

"But Robbie, dear, you can't see if you're sitting on the seat."

"I'll stand!" He jumped into the car and stood up against the window. "Like this, you see? I can see everything perfectly well this way."

"Yes, Robbie. And what happens if the car slams on the brakes? What happens then? You splat against the windshield. And I have either lost, or have a badly damaged, and please note, *extremely expensive*, robot. Robbie, you *must* be in the car seat. It's nonnegotiable. Either get in the car seat or go back into the house." I shoved Robbie over and attached the car seat to the passenger seat.

Robbie stood, swishing his tail.

"Tail swishing will not make any difference. You have to make a choice, and you have to make it now. This is not about you, Robbie, this is about Booji and Evanora. Either get in the car seat, or go back into the house. Or I'll command you to sleep."

"*Not sleep!*" Robbie wailed, reluctantly dragging himself into the car seat. I locked him in place.

"Much better, my friend. You'll be happy once we're in motion. We have an important mission, and I need your help. Besides, it'll be fun!"

"I'm all ready for fun," Robbie grumbled. "Not having fun right now."

He made me guffaw. His over-the-top melodrama struck my funny bone, like it always did. I pulled out my AR glasses and placed them beside me, then threw my backpack on the back seat. "I wonder where we should start looking," I mused.

"Near Evanora's and fan out from there," Robbie suggested.

"Right. A big unspecific, but it's a start. Car, let's go to the forest behind Evanora's."

"To the forest, Dr. Forest," the car quipped.

"Very clever," I replied, amused.

Soon we were on a bumpy, narrow gravel road, with the forest rising up on either side of us. "Windows down," I ordered. The wonderful scent of evergreen and loamy soil wafted over us. "Oh, wow, why don't I come here on occasion?"

"Good question," Robbie said. "It's so close to home, too."

No other cars were on the road and we drove slowly as we peered into the undergrowth, looking for Booji.

An hour later, as lovely and enjoyable as the ride was, I began to feel we were off track. Just as I was about to tell the car to leave the forest, Robbie yelled, "There, Joy, there! In the underbrush, there's a cat."

The car paused.

"I don't see a cat, Robbie," I said, scrutinizing the underbrush.

"Let me outta this thing," Robbie thrashed about with the locking mechanism of the car seat. I reached over and unlocked it. *"Open door!"* Robbie ordered.

The car door opened and Robbie jumped out in a flash.

"Wait! Robbie! Wait!" Alarmed at him flying into the underbrush without any idea of what he might encounter, I threw on my AR glasses, jumped out of the car, and hurried after him. That's when I saw a flash of grey-striped cat hide dive deeper into the underbrush.

"Stay there, Joy," Robbie called to me. "He's scared. You're making him run away."

I stopped, but with concern for Robbie. "Be careful, Robbie. You don't know how he's going to react to you."

Robbie ignored me and went dashing into the thick ferns. I heard a bit of thrashing as he moved, but then, all fell silent. The moments dragged by. I became more and more alarmed. What if Robbie didn't come back?

I thought of Evanora, and how she must be feeling. Awful, dark, and dreadful. I could command Robbie to come back, and I believed he would. But, at the same time, I felt I must let him pursue the grey-striped cat.

I'd give him another minute and then order him to return.

And hope that he would.

The minute crept by.

"*Robbie, return!*" I finally commanded.

He appeared on my wrist comp. "*Shhhh,* Joy," he said in a gentle voice. "I'm talking with the cat now." He showed me the grey kitty, sitting near him, looking frightened and breathing heavily. "I'm trying to convince him to follow me back to you."

"All right," I nodded. "But keep your vid on so I can see what's happening."

Robbie didn't say anything, but he left the image on. At that moment, a car came along the narrow road. I took off my AR glasses and moved back to my car, ready to climb in and pull over—not that there was much of a shoulder to move to, if necessary. The other car found its way around my car, then stopped. A dark-tinted window rolled down.

"Are you all right?" a kindly looking man asked with concern.

"Yes, I'm fine."

"Are you having car trouble?"

"No." I wondered how to tell a complete stranger that my car sat in the middle of a gravel road in the forest because I was waiting for my robot cat to return with a lost bio cat.

Pretty much just like that. "I … ahm, I'm waiting for my robot cat to return with a lost cat that we spied in the forest."

"Oh," the kindly man replied, nodding, as if I'd said the most common and reasonable thing. "Very well. Is it your cat? The bio one, I mean."

"No. We're looking for someone else's cat."

"Good on you, that's very kind! Good day, then."

"Good day! Thanks for stopping."

"No problem." The window roll up and the car drove on.

I looked down at my wrist comp, pleased to see Robbie in motion, and the gray cat with him. Before long, the ferns parted, and the two cats stepped out onto the edge of the road.

The gray cat took one look at me and backed away into the ferns. Robbie said something to him in cat, and he paused.

"Do you think I can approach?"

"I'm not sure, Joy. You can try it. If he bolts, I'll go after him again. I have a firm lock on his bios and I'll be able to find him if necessary."

I moved slowly toward the gray kitty. "Hello pretty kitty. I'd like to take you home. Would you like that?"

He looked at me with caution, but stopped moving away. He then sat down, watching me closely.

Robbie went up to him sort of purr-talking, and sat down beside him. I cautiously moved toward them, also sort of purr-talking. When I got near enough to pet him, I sat down on the moss-covered forest floor.

"Is it okay if I pet you, pretty gray kitty?" I reached out my hand, and the cat didn't move. I petted him, and he appeared to relax.

"I don't think this is Evanora's cat," Robbie said in a quiet voice.

"Why do you say that?"

"Because, first of all, he's a he, and Booji, you've said, is a she."

"Oh! You're right. That slipped my mind."

"And, secondly, even if he were a she, he doesn't look like the picture Evanora showed us."

"*Hmmmm*," I mulled. "I still can't get a bead on the picture she showed us. I couldn't seem to take it in when she brought it up, and I can't recall it now." I continued to stroke the kitty, and he began purring.

"Very good, kitty. Let's go to the car and check out your chip." I gently reached to pick him up, and gave a sigh of relief when he let me. When we were in the car, I closed the doors and put my wrist comp next to his throat. Robbie stood by him, reassuringly.

Soon, data came up, and then, suddenly, a beautiful little girl with long golden hair and stunning blue eyes appeared in the hologram, tears streaming down her face.

"Oh!!" she squealed, *"Do you have Mr. Socks? Do you have my kitty?"*

Chapter 9
Mr. Socks Goes Home

M r. Socks yowled in response.

I glanced down at gray kitty's feet, and, sure enough, he had four pristine white socks. "I believe we do!"

"Thank God!" a woman said, her face coming into view. "I don't know how life could possibly go on here, with Maisie crying nonstop, day and night.

"We went camping last weekend, and Maisie insisted on taking Mr. Socks with us. I told her he would be fine left at home for two days, and the neighbor would check on him. But, without my knowing it, she snuck Mr. Socks into the car. As soon as we unloaded the car at the campsite, the cat, of course, escaped. As you can imagine, that brought about the end of our camping weekend. We've been home doing everything in our power to try to find Mr. Socks.

"*Where* have you found him?"

I showed her my coordinates.

"Oh my goodness! That means the poor little cat has walked something like fifteen or twenty miles in five days, since Saturday, trying to get home."

I looked at the data scrolling beside their faces in the hologram and saw that the address where Mr. Socks lived was yet another fifteen miles. Would he have made it?

I felt so warm and happy about this unanticipated good deed, and smiled at Robbie, who was doing his own version of smiling. "Well, let us get on the road! We'll be there directly."

I closed the connection and let Robbie stay with Mr. Socks in the back of the car. "Don't get used to it! It's back into the car seat after we take Mr. Socks home."

He acted as though he didn't hear me, which I preferred to an irritating argument. Before long, we pulled up to Mr. Sock's charming early twentieth century house, replete with lilac bushes and a little stone path to the door. I saw Maisie's beautiful little face in the front window, as she leaned over the back of the sofa. When we came to a stop, I got out and gathered up Mr. Socks from the back. I heard a squeal from inside the house, with a matching cry from Mr. Socks. Robbie and I hurried up the little stone path, while the door flung open before we even got to it.

Mr. Socks scrabbled about in my arms, and succeeded in escaping. He ran toward the beautiful blond little girl, and they met on the steps.

"Thank you so much," the woman who had talked with me on my wrist comp said, stepping into the doorway. "Come inside, Maisie, bring Mr. Socks inside." Maisie, hugging the cat with all her strength, but Mr. Socks didn't seem to mind, went inside.

"Please come in," Maisie's mother added, "you and your well-behaved cat."

I didn't need to, but I wanted to enjoy more of the bonding between this beautiful little girl and her cat. Robbie and I stepped inside.

Maisie's mother extended her hand, "I'm Jennifer. Please, have a seat," she said, gesturing to the sofa.

I sat on the sofa, and Robbie, not knowing what to do, stood by my feet. I reached down and petted him. "Lovely to meet you and your beautiful daughter, Jennifer. I'm Joy, and this is Robbie."

"Your cat is rather much like a dog, the way he attends to you," she observed.

"He's a robot, and yes, he's very responsive."

"A robot! Do you hear that, Maisie? Her cat is a robot."

Maisie couldn't be bothered to become disengaged with Mr. Socks. "Uh-huh," she said, still tightly hugging her cat.

"It's amazing that you came upon Mr. Socks, out there in the forest. How did that happen?" Jennifer asked.

"Well, interestingly, we were looking for someone else's cat, which is why I had Robbie with me. And good thing, too, because without him I would not have seen Mr. Socks. He spied Maisie's beautiful kitty hiding in the ferns. I pulled over and let Robbie out, and he pursued him until he caught up to him. Then, he convinced Mr. Socks to come with me. His identification chip got me to you."

Jennifer nodded. "I cannot thank you enough. Now maybe things will return to normal around here! We've had a reward out for the retrieval of Mr. Socks, please tell me where I can deposit it."

"Oh no!" I exclaimed. "There's no way in the world I would take a reward for finding and returning your beautiful little girl's kitty. Seeing them together," I gestured to the two of them playing on the floor, so delighted to be reunited, "is more reward than any amount of money."

"Well, we owe you then. Anytime you need a favor, just call on us."

I chuckled. "I can't imagine what that might be, but thank you!" I stood. "I guess we'll be on our way. We still have a cat to find!"

Robbie went over to Maisie and Mr. Socks, said something in cat to his new cat friend, and Mr. Socks replied at length. Maisie's mom and I exchanged a glance. "Perhaps Robbie could come over on occasion and spend a little time with Mr. Socks. They seem to have bonded."

"They do! That's a great idea, to let the cats and Maisie have an occasional play date. What do you think, Maisie?"

She was now hugging both cats, and she looked up at us with her amazing blue eyes aglow. "I love it! I love Robbie! I love you Robbie!" she said hugging him even tighter. "You found my kitty, and you will always be welcome in my home."

Jennifer's eyebrows raised. "My goodness," she whispered, "I've never heard her sound so adult."

"She has a good role model."

"Oh, well, one hopes," Jennifer said shyly.

"Come on, Robbie. We need to find Booji!"

Robbie pulled himself away from the warmth of his new cat and little girl friends. "Bye now," he said.

"Bye," Maisie waved Mr. Socks' paw at us as we left.

Soon, we were back in the car. I headed home to have a bite of lunch and to consider my next move.

"That was so … so … cuddly," Robbie said.

"You really like Mr. Socks and Maisie, don't you?"

"Yes. So much. Who wouldn't?"

"Did you hear Maisie's mother and me agree to let you have an occasional play date with the two of them? How does that sound?"

"It sounds *purrfect*. And … I hope it happens."

"It'll happen."

We soon pulled into the drive at home. Robbie and I went inside and I made myself a peanut butter sandwich and a pot of Ear Grey tea. I eyed the Turkish delight and Evanora's marvelous tea, but resisted, deciding to save them for a treat later.

"I don't quite know what to do now, Robbie. Should we head out again directly? Should we go back to the same location?"

"I suggest waiting until dark, since cats are nocturnal. We might have more luck after dark. And then, yes, I think the territory in or near the forest is a good place to look."

"That's a great idea, if you don't mind coming along again, Robbie. If I were to go out alone in the dark, I'd be even less effective than I was earlier today when you spied Mr. Socks."

Robbie stood up and switched his tail about. "I'll mind if you *don't* take me! Of course I want to come. What we did today was one of the most meaningful events in my life. Seeing Maisie so happy, and making sure that the beautiful Mr. Socks was safe at home, gladdens my robot heart. Let's do it some more!"

"Gladdens your robot heart?" I asked, both amused and touched. "Then we *must* do it some more!"

I puttered about, waiting for dusk to fall. I went out to the garage and put the cat carrier in the car.

Robbie came out with me. "You might as well bring the graphene carrier too."

"Why?"

"Because we may find more than one cat."

"Good point." I called up the graphene cat carrier on my wrist comp, ordering it to come into the back of the car.

Even though I understood the science behind the graphene cat carrier—and all the other graphene things, too—that could float their way to their ordered destination, as well as carry out numerous commands, I still found it pretty darn creepy to see the cat carrier floating off the shelf and into the back of the car, resting beside the other mundane, and far less intelligent, cat carrier.

"It's not quite dark yet, but let's head out. I'd rather be looking than sitting here twiddling our thumbs."

Robbie stood on his hind legs and flung his front legs over his head, waving them about. "No opposable thumbs here, Joy, in case you haven't noticed."

"I've noticed," I said, wincing. It was a particular sore spot with Robbie, as there were many things he could not readily do, lacking the advantage of opposable thumbs. And yet, he complained that if he had opposable thumbs, he would be even less like a real cat, which, in his little robot heart, he longed to be.

"I need to not be sitting here figuratively twiddling my thumbs. I didn't mean to insult you, Robbie, dear."

Slightly mollified, Robbie nodded. "Right. I don't need to watch you figuratively twiddling your thumbs, either. Let's get on the road."

I went back into the house to pet Dickens, who, in his usual spot in the center of the bed, opened one sleepy eye, then closed it again—his version of a blessing.

"Keep the home fires burning, kiddo. Robbie and I will be back … I don't know when … later." I rushed back out to the car, and with much mumbling and grumbling from Robbie, I managed to situate and lock him in the car seat.

Finally, we were ready to hit the road!

I considered stopping by Evanora's place and give her an update, but decided against it, as I had nothing to report about Booji. Except, perhaps, to mention Robbie's particular skill in spotting at least one lost cat. But could he do it again?

"Okay, Car, take us to where we were earlier today, at the outer edge of the forest."

"Yes, Dr. Forest."

We were soon at the edge of the forest where we'd found Mr. Socks. I discovered myself wondering what the heck I was doing. It was now dark, and I was looking for a cat I didn't even know. "Counting on you one-hundred percent here, Robbie. I can't see anything other than the bit of road in the headlights."

"You can count on me, Joy. Remember, I'm your wingman."

We wandered around on the little gravel road for a couple of hours, with not another car on the road, nor a single creature, wild or domestic, stirring in the forest.

I became disheartened. But then I suddenly cried out, *"Oh! Look!"*

Chapter 10
Yellow Tom

Yes! I saw movement among the ferns. The car came to a stop while Robbie and I peered into the underbrush. Everything was still, but then we saw a pair of glowing eyes, watching us intently.

"It's not a cat," Robbie said, disappointed.

"It's not? What is it?"

Casually as the day—or in this case, the night—is long, a raccoon crossed the road in front of us, stopping for a moment to give us a studied glance before disappearing into the forest on the other side of the road.

"Why did the raccoon cross the road?" I asked cryptically.

"I don't know, Joy. Why did the raccoon cross the road?"

"Sorry, Robbie, that's a very, very, very, *very* old joke."

"*Hmmm,*" Robbie mused, clicking audibly through his databanks. Mumbling, "why did the raccoon cross the road? Well, Joy, that doesn't come up. But what *does* come up is, 'why did the *chicken* cross the road?'"

"Yeah, Robbie, that's what my silly reference was refer...."

"*Hey!*" Robbie gestured into the forest some twenty feet ahead of us. "*There is a cat!*"

"Are you sure, Robbie? I can't even make out the ferns."

"Yes," the car said. "Robbie's right, there *is* a feline nearby."

"Let's not scare him," Robbie said. "Stay here—I'll see if I can get close."

"All right, Robbie." I had the car pull to the side of the road, then I released Robbie from of the car seat. He jumped out and scampered ahead of me a few feet, disappearing among the ferns.

I hated seeing him disappear into the forest in the night. I put on my AR glasses then went to the back of the car and directed the graphene cat carrier to wait with me beside the car.

Before long, even though I couldn't see him, Robbie whispered on my wrist comp, "I see him! He's a huge yellow tomcat. He seems very distraught and lost. I'm going to try to befriend him. I hope he takes it in a good way, because he's mighty darn big, and I wouldn't want him to decide he needs to fight me."

"Oh Robbie," I whispered, "please do *not* endanger yourself. If the yellow tomcat is really aggressive, perhaps he's safe here in the forest, with his own combative protection."

Robbie made no reply. I listened intently, hoping not to hear any cat yowling, or hissing, or scratching. Finally I could stand it no more. I adjusted my AR glasses for night vision, and turned on the light beam on my wrist comp, then crept forward, the graphene cat carrier at my side.

As I came near where I thought Robbie had disappeared among the ferns, I turned off the light, moving slowly, listening intently. Finally, I could hear some quiet cat sounds. It sounded like Robbie was having a positive interaction with the yellow tomcat.

I sat down on the side of the road with the cat carrier, tapping out my presence to Robbie. Apparently, the yellow tomcat was not all that easy to convince to come out of the forest. He didn't want to fight, but he also didn't want to come out of his safe spot and probably had no interest in meeting me. And even less than that, would he be inclined to get into a cat carrier?

"Patience is a virtue," I reminded myself silently. But myself wasn't inclined to listen.

Moments. Ticked. By.

But, finally, I heard a rustling among the ferns, although I still could barely see anything in the total darkness, even with my AR glasses. Then, through the ferns came an enormous yellow cat, clearly visible, even in the darkness. Robbie followed him closely, looking more cat-like then I'd ever seen him, their long strides matched. They could just as well be on the African veld.

They were still about eight feet distant, when the yellow tomcat saw me. He sat down on his haunches, and gave me a considered look—not about to bolt, but not about to continue coming toward me, either. Robbie sat next to him.

Something in me told me to gesture to the cat to come to me, so I extended my hand. Much to my surprise, the gigantic cat leapt up and flew toward me. I braced myself. I didn't have time to stand up, and I had no idea what the cat was about to do.

What he did was climb into my lap and start purring. I was stunned! I wrapped my arms around him, and said softly, "everything is all right yellow kitty, everything is all right."

Robbie had run alongside the cat as he sprang toward me, to protect me if necessary. He was as surprised as I was. "Oh, Joy, what a thing to see! This poor cat has had a hard time of it. His people, the people that he'd spent his whole life with for years, brought him out here to the forest and dropped him off. They abandoned him. They broke his heart."

Almost nothing ever made me cry. But this did! "Poor kitty, poor beautiful kitty! We will find someone to love you like you deserve, don't you worry!"

"Or we could keep him!" Robbie said.

"We could, but I'm pretty much at my cat quota, Robbie. He's an excellent, and gorgeous, and exceedingly sweet cat. There's someone who needs this beautiful cat as much as he needs someone. We'll leave our options open."

"I like him, Joy. I really like him. He's a very wise cat. I cannot imagine what is wrong with humans who abandon members of their family that they've contracted with God and nature to care for, just because they have fur or feathers."

"Oh, Robbie, I couldn't agree with you more. But humans also abandon humans. It's beyond comprehension. However, we'll do our part. We'll do what we can to make things better for people or creatures who come our way and need help." I hugged the yellow tomcat, and he purred yet louder, if possible.

"We won't be needing the cat carrier to get him into the car," I said standing awkwardly while holding the very large cat. "Cat carrier, follow," I said. Robbie, cat carrier, and I moved to the back to the car.

I opened the back of the car and put the yellow tomcat down in order to open the carrier. "I don't suppose there's even any point in checking his chip—if he has one—it will only tell us about the people who abandoned him. And I'd rather not know anything about them."

"True. Terrible, terrible people. I'd better never find out who they are! I'll … I'll short circuit their computers!" Robbie growled, angry in a way I'd never seen him angry.

"Oh! Goodness! You could probably do that, too, if you absolutely decided to!"

"I could," Robbie said in a matter-of-fact voice.

"Let's just focus on the yellow tomcat right now, and let karma attend to his former owners," I said, patting Robbie on the head.

"So, dear yellow tomcat," I said, turning my attention to the orphan, "I need you to ride in this cat carrier for the sake of your own safety." I started to put him in the carrier but he was not having it. He put his gigantic paws on either side of the doorway, and without fighting or growling or scratching, he flatly refused to got into the carrier.

"He's suffered enough trauma," Robbie said. "I bet the last time he saw a cat carrier was the last time he saw his people."

"Yes," I agreed, wondering why I hadn't thought of that myself. "No doubt you're right, Robbie." I held the cat in my arms. "Okay then, Yellow Tom," I said christening him, "I guess you'll have to ride on the front seat with us, but you must be good and sit still." I closed up the back of the car and we all moved to the front seat.

"I need to sit on the seat with him," Robbie insisted.

"No, you don't, Robbie," I took off my AR glasses. "I can't be worrying about two creatures flying about in case of an accident."

"We're not going to have an accident," Robbie argued.

"I certainly hope not! But that doesn't change the fact that you're going to be in the car seat without further argument. And if not, as you know, I can have you go to...."

"Not sleeeeep!" Robbie whined as he climbed into the car seat.

"Much better, thank you!" I made sure he was secure.

Yellow Tom sat calmly, watching our exchange.

"All right now, back home. One more cat, but still no Booji." The thought crossed my mind that, perhaps, if I could not find Booji maybe Evanora would consider taking the most excellent Yellow Tom into her life.

However, I didn't need to contemplate that at this moment. Given how readily we found cats, I still hoped we'd find Booji.

"We'll still keep our eyes open on the drive home for Booji," I said aloud.

"Oh, Right! We need to find Booji," Robbie said. "I'm too preoccupied with Yellow Tom."

We slowly crept out of the forest, keeping our eyes on both sides of the road, peering into the thick forest.

As we came out of the forest onto the main road, a huge, glowing light overhead lit up the interior of the car. The car slammed on the brakes while, terrified, Yellow Tom let out a mighty screech, and dove into the back of the car.

Chapter 11
Flying Man

The Space XXX Roadster floated down onto the road in front of me as I pulled to the side of the road.

"It's all right, Yellow Tom," I called to the terrorized cat. I looked over my shoulder, but couldn't see him.

"*Holy guacamole,*" Robbie said, so stunned, he defaulted to using one of my exclamations.

"Yeah. Holy guacamole," I agreed. I watched Travis climb out of the flying car and stride back to us.

It did not hurt my eyes in the least. He belonged on the cover of the Clark County Police Force calendar, although I don't think there is one. But … there ought to be.

"What are you doing out at this hour, young lady?" He asked, grinning, as he came up to my car window.

"Finding cats," I said.

"Evanora succeeded in recruiting you?"

"Yes, she did, with a little arm twisting from my friend here." I gestured to Robbie.

Travis flashed a light into the car, blinding both of us.

"*Wah! Wah! Wah*," Robbie cried.

"*Arg*, Travis! Do you have to blind us?"

"Sorry!"

"You already scared the wits out of the Yellow Tom we found, when you invaded us from overhead. He made a dive for the back. I need to find him, and calm him down."

"Yeah," Travis said, peering into the back. "I can see some movement under the back seat. There's a big fluffy yellow striped tail sticking out and wagging about."

"Oh! Poor kitty. He's had a terrible time. His people brought him out here and dumped him off in the forest."

Travis laughed. "The cat told you that, did he?"

"He told Robbie."

Travis smirked. "Your robot cat had a conversation with a yellow tomcat. I'm sure."

"*What* are you smirking about? I'm sure he did, too. But you're *not* sure that he did. You're … you're making fun of us. I guess you've forgotten who you're talking with."

The smirky smile left Travis's face. "Well, yes, I think I did forget who I was talking with." He leaned down and put his forearms on the edge of my rolled-down window, and addressed Robbie. "Good job robot, saving an actual real live cat."

"Thanks," Robbie said in a cold voice, without looking at Travis.

Oh no, I thought, something not good was about to happen. I knew Robbie already did not like Travis, and for good reason. Travis seemed to have to poke at Robbie, insulting him, and hurting his feelings. An unattractive trait.

And, sure enough, Travis launched right into it. "So, I see you're in the baby seat. Looking forward to graduating out of it are you? Not likely!"

"Travis!" I reprimanded, a bit shocked, a bit furious. "Why in the name of Anubis must you harass my companion?"

"Companion! He's a robot, Joy. *A robot.*"

"A robot with bios, a robot with sophisticated, and I might add, very expensive AI components. Robbie experiences true emotions, as I see it. Insulting and belittling him means that I have to deal with it. He will ruminate on your abuse, and I have to hear it. I have to make it better. Seriously, I have no comprehension what it is about my Robbie that makes you behave like a high school freshman."

Travis stood up and looked down at me, reading me. I could see he was trying to determine if I was being facetious or serious. Most frustrating! Given that we've had conversations along this line before when I've asked him to talk respectfully to Robbie.

He seemed to figure out that yes indeed, I was serious.

"Sorry, Joy. I didn't mean to upset you. And, I guess I have to add that I didn't mean to upset Robbie."

"Please understand, Travis, Robbie learns nonstop. His greatest influence is me. Much of who Robbie is, is a reflection of who I am, and I guess what I'm saying is: if you insult my cat, you've insulted me."

"I see that now," Travis acquiesced.

Startling everyone, Yellow Tom jumped up on the back of the car seat between Robbie and me. I reached up and pulled him into my lap. "Here we are, beautiful cat, Travis is sorry he has disrupted everyone and either scared or insulted us. Or both."

I couldn't help it. Suddenly, everything seemed so strange and ridiculous, I burst out laughing. Both Travis and Robbie looked at me like I had lost a few screws. And perhaps I had. This cat hunting, this crazy long day, had worn me down.

"I'm glad to see that you still have your sense of humor," Travis observed. "Although I'm not exactly sure what you're laughing at."

"Me neither, Travis!"

"So, now that the mood is shifted—not entirely sure how or why—I'll get back to the point I meant to make when I first saw you out here in the night on the edge of the forest."

"You have a point?…"

"I do. My shift is almost over. I thought I'd ask if you'd like to grab a bite to eat."

I looked at the dash, it was, *somehow!*, three a.m. "Where exactly did you have in mind to go at three a.m.?"

"The only place that's open that has decent food is *24 Hour Breakfast*."

I reflected on the times we'd sparred around with the idea of going out to dinner, and what a far cry *24 Hour Breakfast* was from a nice dinner at a pleasant venue. But, still fully frustrated with Travis, I wanted to give him a slightly bigger piece of my mind, without Robbie present.

"Sounds delightful," I couldn't resist an edge of sarcasm. "Let me drop off the kids, and I'll meet you there in half an hour."

"Setting aside your sarcastic tone, I'll accept your enthusiasm and meet you there." He turned and walked back to the Space XXX Roadster, calling over his shoulder, "Sorry Robbie!"

Travis receding was also not a bad view—he certainly knew how to make a uniform look its best. Even in my low-grade-steaming-almost-anger I couldn't resist appreciating the view.

Call me sexiest if you will, but, IMHO, a gorgeous man is a pleasure to behold.

The Space XXX Roadster lifted off and disappeared into the starry night sky.

I took a few moments to enjoy the stars, a sight I could not see from my house, with Yellow Tom curled up in my lap, purring softly. I hated to disturb him, but I finally gently set him beside me on the car seat. He looked up at me, and purred yet more resoundingly.

"Home, James," I ordered the car.

"Yes, Dr. Forest."

Sailing along in the lovely evening, Robbie dropped a bombshell.

Chapter 12

Three Cats

"I don't like Travis," Robbie said.

Not a bombshell, exactly. I knew how he felt, but that he voiced a strong negative opinion, completely his own, was a new level of personality from his AI.

Although I needed to give some thought to this development, I attempted to carry on the conversation as though I found it completely normal. "Fortunately, Robbie, you don't have to like Travis. It'd be nice if you did, but you don't have to."

"*You don't have to either,*" Robbie observed adding a low growl.

"True! But I *want* to. I *want* to like Travis. Even though he can be as thick as a Roman wall at times."

"Yeah, thick. And Just. Plain. Rude." I heard his claws dig into the frame of the car seat, then relax. "I like Myles."

"I like Myles too. But he comes with his own baggage."

"He does?"

"He does." I thought again about my affirmation to not let Myles break my heart a second time.

I felt Robbie looking at me. I kept my eyes on the road. "Tell me more."

"I'm not going to go into that right now, Robbie. I'm preoccupied with the stuff going on in the present moment. But … suffice it to say, he has a wife who is not 'ex' yet. If ever. And he has a daughter."

"But … I thought you liked his daughter. Blaze. I thought you liked her."

"I do like her, Robbie. I like her very much. I may actually like her more than Myles."

"*Hmmm,*" Robbie said reflecting. "Well then, that's good. But I guess the fact that somewhere he has a wife, I guess that's not good."

"You got it Robbie. Not good. Especially when she's on my very short list of people I do not like, and even more to the point, I completely do not trust her."

"Does that mean then, that you don't trust Myles, too?"

"Not so much don't trust him, like he's bad, but, I'm not sure that he knows what he thinks." The car pulled into the driveway. "In any case, this discussion is better had some other time. Let's take Yellow Tom inside."

I released Robbie from his despised restriction. Then I picked up Yellow Tom, and we all went inside.

I had to think about what I was going to say to Travis. No, scratch that. I had to think about the fact that Travis had come down out of the sky, specifically to ask me to go "grab a bite to eat."

I wondered what went through his mind when he saw a car coming out of the forest at three a.m. and then realized it was me. It must've seemed strange. Certainly unanticipated. And he reacted. He could've flown on by, he could've connected with my wrist comp and asked me what I was doing, coming out of the forest in the wee hours.

But he came down out of the sky, and walked up to me ... and, unfortunately, there the picture kind of loses its romantic charm. I felt my frustration with him rising up again. *Really!* Why did he have to insult Robbie? It could've been such a lovely moment.

"Now," the wiser, calmer, more mature voice in my head said, "Let it go. You can just let it go. There's no advantage to indulging in this anger. It doesn't hurt Travis the least, but it takes a toll on me."

"Yeah! But! He started it!" the considerably less mature voice in my head argued. "I would've been perfectly happy to be invited to some less than stellar twenty-four-hour breakfast place, and I'd be in a very different frame of mind at this moment if he hadn't picked on Robbie."

"True," the wise woman responded. "But, again, the toll you're allowing his comments to take, only hurts myself."

I shook my head trying to clear it. "I'll take this head-talk under advisement," I said out loud, knowing full well I was about to give Travis a piece of my mind, and probably even before having a sip of tea.

I considered the two cats that I brought into the house. Looking down, I saw Robbie studying me intently, and, in fact, so was Yellow Tom.

"All right you guys, I've got to get going. I'll get to *24 Hour Breakfast* and Travis will be gone. All of this head talk between my ego and super ego will be over nothing."

"Head talk," Robbie said. "I see. I wondered what was going on with you."

"Let's go into the bedroom and get Yellow Tom settled." Oh no, I suddenly thought, Yellow Tom and Dickens might not get along. I needed to find out about that immediately.

The three of us trooped into the bedroom. Predictably, Dickens slept in the center of the bed, curled up like a fuzzy little caterpillar. I picked up Yellow Tom and sat on the edge of the bed with him in my arms.

"You see this other kitty here, Mr. Yellow Tom? Now, he's kind of lazy, but we love him, and I hope you will too." I reached out and petted Dickens, who cracked an eye to look at me.

Yellow Tom left my lap and moved over to Dickens. I braced myself for just about anything. Because if Yellow Tom decided to get aggressive it would be difficult for everyone in the room. If such a huge cat decided to fight, all of us would hardly be a match for him.

But he cautiously sniffed at Dickens, who raised his head and looked at Yellow Tom. Then they touched noses, and I heard audible purring from both of them.

Robbie jumped up on the bed to join us. "*Wow!* That's fantastic! I'm thinking that kind of warm fuzzy is not usual between two tomcats who are just meeting."

"I'm thinking you're right. I felt cautious, although there's not much tomcat left in Dickens. Still, this is a big relief."

Then Yellow Tom curled up next to Dickens, continuing to purr. Robbie jumped up on the bed and joined them. I stood and grin down at the three of them together. What an incredibly sweet, adorable sight.

"Okay, kids, sleep tight. I'll be back in a while."

"Make sure you are!" Robbie said.

"Oh! Getting parental now are you? I've already stayed out long past my curfew." Chuckling I left the bedroom, glancing at my reflection as I passed the mirror, I saw an exhausted, and somewhat scruffy woman.

Well, ya gets what I gots, I thought. I couldn't waste any more time on … whatever I might have done to make myself more presentable, had I been asked out in a reasonable manner and in a reasonable time frame.

I scurried through the house and back to the car. *"24 Hour Breakfast,"* I told the car.

"Right. Breakfast at three-thirty a.m."

"What exactly, are you saying to me?"

"Nothing, Dr. Forest, other than making the observation that you've never gone out to breakfast at three-thirty a.m. that I know of."

"Great memory banks. What you say is true. But how about let's just get me there before it gets any later?"

"Of course," Dr. Forest.

We soon pulled in to the parking lot of *24 Hour Breakfast*. Not only had I never been here, but I hadn't known exactly where it was. It was considerably closer to home than I imagined. How could I have missed it? Given that I rarely eat breakfast of any sort might have something to do with it, I re-minded myself.

I looked around for the Space XXX Roadster, but it was not to be seen.

Disappointment washed over me.

24 Hour Breakfast

Chapter 13
24 Hour Breakfast

That's what you get, I thought, for standing around talking to yourself and complaining about Travis instead of just coming to meet him. You missed him.

I might as well go back home. But I felt so antsy and irritated that I got out of the car and leaned against it. I had my back to *24 Hour Breakfast*, but I turned to study it, with the rather superficial thought that I might go check it out, as long as I was here. But I didn't feel like doing that, either.

The front of the restaurant was plastered with vintage-looking garish neon signs of all stripes and hues, declaring "breakfast" in a plethora of languages. At least, that's what I figured the languages I don't know were saying, as that's what the languages I do have a passing understanding of declared, all hovering around a gigantic sign that visually blared:

BREAKFAST—24 HOURS

EAT YOUR NATIVE BREAKFAST

WITH THE FOLKS BACK HOME!

I turned away from the glut of visual overload. I hated this feeling of ambivalence. Should I stay? Should I go? It was so unlike me, and I didn't like me of the moment. What was up with me?

I was angry with myself, yes. And, riding on the coattails of my anger with Travis, I was just sort of a big ole pile of anger. But I'd been awake around twenty-two hours—*and a strange twenty-two hours*—I was in no condition to deal with my own unpleasant, atypical, emotions. Look, I thought pragmatically, you have a new kitty at home who needs looking after. *So go home!*

That ended my ambivalence. I turned and started to get back into the car, when the Space XXX Roadster sighed down from the sky and rested beside me.

Travis climbed out and ambled over to me. "Sorry I'm late, Joy. Got an emergency call right after talking with you. Why didn't you go on inside?"

"I've never been here. I was trying to decide if I wanted to go in if you weren't here. I just got here myself. I figured you'd come and gone."

He put his hand lightly on my back, and we walked to the front entrance. "I wouldn't do that, Joy!"

"Good to know," I noted.

We stepped through the entrance of *24 Hour Breakfast*.

"*Wow!*" I said softly, taking in the surroundings. Contrary to the garish exterior, the lighting was muted. The interior was a huge, huge circle, with bustling waitresses and cooks in an inner circle. On the wall around the outside edge were clocks at regular intervals, each an hour ahead or behind those on either side of it.

A menu under every clock scrolled the cultural breakfast favorites of that part of the world. The place was pretty quiet with a few East Coast looking types —whatever that means—under a six-thirty a.m. clock. The place was otherwise pretty empty. Not so many people living in the Atlantic Ocean, I surmised.

"What sort of breakfast are you in the mood for?" Travis asked.

I looked up at the menu by where I stood. It featured synthetic whale blubber. I felt my stomach do a bit of a somersault.

"I think a bowl of oatmeal with some blueberries on it sounds about right at the moment."

"That's not very experimental."

"After being awake nearly around the clock, experimental is the last thing I'm feeling." Then I remembered that Travis had come to my place yesterday morning when Evanora breached my security system.

"I guess it's probably the same for you, given that you were at my place early yesterday morning."

"I had a 24 hour day *yesterday*. When I responded to the security breach at your place, that was the end of two back-to-back shifts. We're shorthanded lately."

"Or always." I observed.

"Or always, yeah. Anyway, I had a solid five hours sleep this afternoon."

"Does that mean you're in an experimental breakfast mood?" I feared what he might be inclined to want to scoff down.

"Sort of. They have these synthetic squid parts that are...." He took in my expression. "I know it sounds awful, but don't knock it till you've tried it. I don't think it's the fake squid as much as the amazing sauce that accompanies it."

"I'm sticking to my oatmeal and blueberries, if it's all the same to you."

"Sure. Oatmeal and squid parts. All righty, you sit down right here, and I'll bring it all back. We have to wait on ourselves. The oatmeal is over here, and the squid parts are over there." He gestured vaguely.

I looked at the cozy booth near me, in muted light and no one else nearby, and thought his suggestion sounded like a really good idea. Yep! I would let him wait on me. "I'll just be right here, then," I said, hunkering down in the booth.

Travis nodded. "Don't go anywhere," he teased.

"The only place I might go," I said, "is to sleep."

"Don't do that! I'll be right back."

I watched as he went off to the circle in the center and around the edge of it where I could not see him. I just now noticed that he had changed into street clothes. How did I not notice that before? I'd not often seen him in street clothes, and I had to say that he did as much justice to them as he did his uniform.

I also have to say that finding a man attractive is quite disruptive when you're trying to be angry with him.

Much to my chagrin, I did, indeed, fall asleep. The next thing I knew, I felt Travis gently tapping me on the shoulder, with the warm aroma of oatmeal wafting up into my receded consciousness. I didn't know which I liked better, his warm touch or the warmth of the oatmeal, but they were both pretty dang sweet to wake up to.

I sat up, stifled a yawn, and looked across at his fake sea creature parts. Yikes and yuck! The pile of tentacles looked entirely too authentic. At least there was no mercury poisoning in it, and at least the real creatures were left to try to not become extinct. Two good points. Still, giving his plate another glance, nope, not something I felt the least bit inclined to try.

"I brought you a glass of oat milk. I think I remember you like oat milk."

"I do," I said surprised that he remembered such a small detail, and wondering when I told him that. I can't even remember telling him, and he remembers it. Pretty impressive. I poured a bit of milk on my oatmeal. The blueberries were huge. I picked one up and popped it in my mouth. *Yum! Delicious!*

I launched into my oatmeal, avoiding taking in Travis wolfing down the tentacles.

And then I remembered that I was mad at him. That little voice said, let it go. But no, I wasn't going to. I didn't want there to be any more interactions between Robbie and Travis like the one we had tonight.

"Travis, I have a bone to pick with you...." I started.

The little smile he wore while engaged in the pleasure of his breakfast, faded. He stopped chewing, and a stormy cloud took over his features. *"What?..."*

24 Hour Breakfast

Chapter 14
You're Beautiful Too

O h, *what* was the matter with me? Here we were, having a perfectly lovely time, sort of, with me half asleep, and I had to destroy the mood.

I decided to attempt to backpedal. "Please don't stop eating. That was not a particularly graceful approach on my part. But ... I'm still feeling upset about the interaction between you and Robbie."

Travis resumed eating, which I took as a good sign. "Well, Joy, I did apologize to you. And I even apologized to Robbie."

"You did, Travis, that's true. And I hope you meant it."

"Of course I meant it," Travis said, with a testy edge in his voice.

Oh dear, this was not going well. Was I now the person who had to make an apology? I felt a bit cornered. Not good. I asked my wise woman voice inside how best to handle the situation—I wanted our pleasant moment to return. But she remained silent. I was on my own.

"I'm glad to hear that, Travis. Because after you left, the first thing Robbie said was, 'I don't like Travis.' I've never heard him decide for himself about liking or not liking someone. I'm concerned that it will negatively influence his AI, overall.

"Really Travis, it's like being a parent to a human child. He's learning rapidly, *ahm*, paw over claw, I guess I'd say, rather than hand over fist, and I don't want a neural pathway laid down that at core doesn't like you. Will it affect him in other ways?

"He keeps my life in order. He contains all of my writing, he retains all of my dictated musings, he has all of my household business, which alone I can't ever seem to keep in order. He pays the bills, he sorts through my email, he's a component of my personal and house security. So forth and so on.

"And surprisingly, he does physical things as well. He's much more useful and integrated in my life than I first ever knew could happen. He feeds Dickens, he kind of cleans up around the house—at least to the extent of his ability." I chuckled, thinking about his incessant complaints about not having opposable thumbs.

Travis's stormy expression melted into one of curiosity.

"I'm chuckling because he's constantly complaining about not having opposable thumbs. But, then he complains, if he had them, he'd not be like a cat."

"He cares if he's like a cat?"

"Yes. He does. Robbie is quite intelligent and quite emotional. And, you see Travis, not only do I love him the way he is, but even if I were to somehow, pragmatically, let us say, determine I should have a less emotional robot assistant, it would be a huge project to get some other robot to know and to do everything Robbie does.

"Of course, he can be downloaded into another robot, but would it be the same with all the services and assistance Robbie provides? Completely ignoring the companionable aspect of having him in my life.

"Well, it's not a place I intend to go. Robbie is backed up into a vault every few minutes. So, if somehow I should lose him, all the data is safe, but would I lose the essential Robbie?" I paused.

"Hopefully, Travis, you understand why I have no desire to have to find out. When you left us there on the forest road, it caused me serious consternation when he said he didn't like you. Then he said he likes Myles, and so I had to have a talk with him about Myles."

"Myles?"

I actually managed to make him stop eating again.

"Your friend from home?"

"Yes. My friend from home," I nodded. Oh boy, I sure didn't want to get into Myles now with Travis. "So, I had to explain to Robbie that Myles is still married, and, anyway, let's not get into that right now. I'll just stick with the point I'm trying to make, which is, simply, please, Travis, don't poke at Robbie. And please don't be upset with me because I ask."

Travis nodded thoughtfully. "That was quite a lot of information, Joy, and also, pretty interesting. Of course, I'm not upset with you for asking me to not tease your robot cat. I had no idea so much was going on. But about Myles...."

"No, let's not talk about Myles." And then, the burning question I had leapt into my mind. "But here's an interesting question ... that energy between you and Evanora yesterday morning ... why have you not had an interest in her? She's fascinating, intelligent, kind, and pretty."

Travis actually put down his fork. He raised an eyebrow and nodded. "Pretty, yes. Actually, beautiful. Those violet eyes...."

Swallowing something inside me that I didn't like, was it jealousy?—you started it, I said to myself. "Yes, beautiful. And those violet eyes."

"But you, too, are beautiful, Joy. And fascinating, intelligent, and kind. You're kind of direct sometimes, but ultimately it's a trait I admire—even when I have to experience it first hand." He sort of chuckled.

"I… *ahm*… I," words failed me. "Ah, *hmmm*, well, thank you, Travis. I didn't know you.…"

At that moment, Travis looked beyond me toward the doorway, then put his hand to his forehead. "Oh, no.…"

24 Hour Breakfast

Chapter 15
Breakfast Interruptus

I looked over my shoulder and saw Bruno, a peer detective of Travis. An irritating, pushy, pudgy, short man. My reaction was identical to Travis's. I put my hand to my forehead and shook my head, looking down into what was left of my cold oatmeal.

Whatever moment Travis and I had been having, it was now over.

"*Hey!*" Bruno said, coming up to us. "When I saw the Space XXX Roadster outside, I said to myself, great! A breakfast companion." He leered at me. "But what a frickin' bonus! Joy, too!"

"That's Dr. Forest to you," I said.

He chuckled about a dozen decibels too loud and plopped his pudgy self down beside me. "Funny girl! You don't mind if I sit beside you, do you?"

"Yes."

He let out his irritating laugh again and put his arm around my shoulders. I frowned up at Travis.

"Bruno, what are you doing?" Travis said in a quiet, no-nonsense voice. "Take your hands off Joy."

"*Oh-ho*, possessive!"

Travis gave him a thunderous look.

"All right, all right," he removed his arm, but didn't bother to put any space between us. "Don't handcuff me for showing a bit of innocent affection for a friend I haven't seen in a while."

I turned my frown to face Bruno. "Friends? Since when are we friends?"

"Oh, now I'm hurt. I'm truly hurt," he said without sounding the least bit offended. "You remember that office party a couple years ago, when you chatted me up."

That 'party' wasn't so much a party as a professional function that I attended because I was doing research around a local ethnic group that had been profiled. Bruno had been instrumental in discovering details of the abuse. I hadn't "chatted him up," I'd been doing my job. But, what can you do about someone like Bruno, submerged in his own reality?

I scooched away from him in the booth and took my oatmeal with me. I poured a bit more oat milk on it, stirred it up, and ate it cold. *Wow!* It still tasted pretty darn good!

Bruno had the unmitigated gall to scooch up against me again.

"If you don't mind!" I said, sliding over the last two inches I had in the booth. "I'm trying to eat my breakfast. Kindly please grant me some elbow room."

"Bruno!" Travis reprimanded, "will you stop harassing Joy?"

"I'm not harassing her. I'm not harassing you, am I, Joy? We're just having some fun."

"Not having fun," I affirmed quietly. "Yes, you're harassing me."

"Oh my goodness, her royal highness. *Excuuuse* me, HRH."

I rolled my eyes at Travis, then returned my attention to my oatmeal, polished it off, and finished my milk. Clearly, my moment with Travis was irreparably damaged.

Bruno reached across and stole one of the tentacles off of Travis's plate.

"Hey!" Travis squawked, slapping Bruno's hand with his fork, then realizing he hadn't wanted to touch Bruno's hand with his fork. I had one in the rolled up napkin of silver he'd brought me, and I handed it to him. "Thanks."

Bruno, oblivious to the nuances going on between Travis and me, continued. "Yeah, I'm on a missing person's case. I got a near hysterical call from that woman that has a thing for you. You know, that woman who just about anyone would give their eye-teeth to have a chance to play with, and you sort of wouldn't even give her the time of day, beyond your professional duties? Evanora."

Oh my goodness!—Evanora between Travis and me again! But wait, I thought. She called about....

"Birdie," Bruno said. "Birdie, her roommate, she said. She said her roommate has been gone for three or four days, and she wasn't too worried about her, but now her pendulum told her that something was seriously wrong. And that Birdie was in trouble." Bruno made some kind of horrible sucking, laughing sound, and then almost choked on the tentacle he'd stolen.

"*Augggh, criminy*, Travis, you trying to kill me?"

"You stole my food. Looks like karma to me."

"Anyway, here I am, in the dead of night, looking for a woman named Birdie because a pendulum said she's in trouble, when I stumble on the Space XXX Roadster. Cool enough! But catching you two in a *tête-à-tête*! Frosting on the ridiculous-hour cake."

"You haven't caught us at anything, Bruno," I said, not even trying to disguise my disgust. "*Sheesh!* You have no boundaries."

"*He he he!* You're easy to rile."

"Not really. Did Evanora give you any concrete information regarding what she thought about where a Birdie might be, or what might have happened to her?"

"No. I think the two of them had a quarrel, and Birdie flew away for a while. Evanora mentioned she hired you to look for her cat. All pretty interesting, no? Both Evanora's cat and Birdie are at large."

I couldn't argue with him on that point. This thought had played around in my mind all day. Yesterday, that is. But Bruno had returned me to my own reality. I needed to get back on the road to look for Booji. But, I *had* to have some sleep before I could be fully functional. I waved my hand at Bruno, gesturing for him to get up so I could escape the booth.

"I gotta get home. I've got a new cat that needs attention. I gotta get some sleep. I gotta find another cat. Thank you for the lovely breakfast, Travis."

Bruno finally managed to struggle his way out of the booth. I slid across and stood. He could not resist putting his hands on me one more time. At his full shoe-lift height, he almost came to my chin. He gave me a gigantic, unwanted bear hug. "So good to see you, Joy. Don't be a stranger!"

"Right!" I exclaimed. "You're strange enough."

"Ha-ha, funny girl,"

"I'll walk you to your car," Travis began to stand.

"Don't bother, Travis, he'll just eat the rest of your breakfast."

"True! But I've rather lost my appetite, anyway."

I turned and exited, not sure if Travis followed me. He did.

We seemed to have nothing to say on the short walk to my car, so pleasantly comfortable. "Well," I said when I got to the passenger side of my car, "thanks again for breakfast. Lovely blueberries and delicious oatmeal. I think it's the best oatmeal I've ever had. Sorry about … my … *ahm*, aggression."

"That's okay, Joy. I now have a better understanding about your relationship with Robbie. And, well, I've been a jerk."

"No, no! That's too strong," I protested. Then I had a second thought.

"Well, maybe a wee bit of a jerk!"

We both giggled. "Open," I commanded the car, and the door opened. "I *must* have a couple hours sleep, and then out to look for Booji again. I'm particularly concerned about Birdie, now, though. Evanora was tremendously upset today ... *urg*, I mean yesterday. See, I need sleep."

Travis wordlessly folded me in his arms for a few seconds, then turned and walked back to *24 Hour Breakfast*. "Sweet dreams," he called over his shoulder. "And give Robbie a hug from me."

I laughed. "He'll ... love that!" I climbed into the car.

"Home James."

"Yes, Dr Forest."

I had just about fallen asleep on the few minutes' ride home, when Robbie's holo came, full-life, into the car, in bright lights.

"What's wrong?"

Over a horrible, undefinable noise, Robbie cried, *"Come home! Come home now!"*

Chapter 16
Transmogrification!

"I'm almost there! What's going on?"
Robbie showed me what he saw. In my bedroom stood the life-sized holo of Evanora.

I like the woman well enough, but this was too much.

"She's crying and turning into different ... beings, I guess." Even as he spoke, I watched Evanora transmogrify from her recognizable self into some sort of less than charming bridge troll. All the while sobbing and wailing.

I pulled the car into the drive. "Oh, for the love of Hades, can I have no peace?"

"It would seem not," the car answered.

"Thank you, Car. I was being rhetorical." I jumped out and flew through the back door, across the kitchen, and into my bedroom. Robbie stood facing the gigantic holo, larger than life-sized. And metamorphosing again, from the bridge troll to the little girl who had cried on my sofa.

"*Evanora!* Why are you projecting your holo into my bedroom?"

"*Oh! Joy! Joy!* I don't know what to do. Booji is gone! Birdie is gone! I'm completely beside myself."

I almost laughed. It was literally true. The "beside herself" entity floated, taking up a large portion of my bedroom. I looked over at the bed to see how Dickens and Yellow Tom were taking this frightening phenomenon. They were not to be seen. If Dickens was not on the bed, that meant they were pretty darn well frightened.

"Evanora, you *must* calm down. And you *must* remove your holo from my bedroom. You have frightened my creatures. That's not all right. I've been awake twenty-four hours now. I have to get a little nap before I go looking for Booji again.

"In addition, Bruno and Travis are looking for Birdie. Everyone is doing everything they can, and you must not tap our resources, especially mine. Now please remove your holo and go to sleep."

"But Birdie and I have a safe word. Since we do crash into loggerheads on occasion, we agreed to have a safe word. And if we use the safe word, then we have to let go of our anger. I used the safe word, and she has not responded. This is very alarming. She wouldn't do that."

"What is the safe word?" I asked.

"We've come to loggerheads."

"Yes," I acknowledged. "But what's the safe word?"

"We've come to loggerheads," Evanora said with irritation.

"Sorry Evanora, I didn't understand. We've come to loggerheads. What a great safe word—or sentence, actually," I said, a bit sincere, a bit sarcastic.

"Anyway," Evanora carried on, "she has not responded, and she wouldn't do that. Something is really, really, *really*, wrong."

"The police are looking for her," I reassured her. "If she's around here, I'm sure they'll find her soon. But perhaps she's traveled somewhere else, and doesn't want to talk to you for a while."

"No. She would never not respond to our safe word, unless something is really…" she started to cry, and the energy around her swirled. I feared she would change form again. "And Booji is still missing, and I just can't take it all."

"You must remain calm, Evanora. There are many creatures who depend on you to take care of them. Please do that and let those of us who are taking care of things for you do what we must do. If I feel like I need to come and be with you, then I'm not looking for Booji."

"But, Joy, the pendulum says…."

"The pendulum let us know we need to step up our efforts. And that's being done. Please! Let everyone do what we can without disrupting our efforts. Right now, you're doing more harm than good by keeping me from getting a little bit of sleep."

"How can you possibly sleep, Joy, when these precious beings are missing?"

The fact of the matter was that I feared I'd have an extremely difficult time getting any sleep for the very reason that I'd become quite alarmed about both Booji and Birdie's disappearance. "Even if I can't sleep, I must try. I must at least relax. It's been an intense, a *very intense* twenty-four hours. I will talk to you in three or four hours. Go out and talk to Heady and the other creatures—let them calm you. Everything will be all right."

I didn't know if that was true, but I didn't know that it wasn't true, either. It seemed the best approach for the moment, because the holo before me of the sobbing, grief stricken Evanora began to fade.

In a small voice she said, "All right, Joy all right." The wild reds and oranges swirling around her calmed down to muted peach and pink. "I must take care of Heady and all the creatures. You're absolutely right. But I'm waiting on tenterhooks until I hear from you. Sleep well!"

And she disappeared.

With a deep sigh, I got down on my hands and knees and looked under the bed. That was my first mistake! There was a little village under there, and I simply did not have the time, the energy, or the patience to sort it out.

I sat up on my knees and looked over at Robbie. "What's under my bed, Robbie?"

"What do you mean?" he asked in his butter-wouldn't-melt-in-his-mouth-innocent-as-the-day-is-long voice.

"You know what I mean. Oh Robbie! I'm wiped out right now. I can't deal with this."

"Well then, Joy, don't." He came over and patted me on the shoulder. "I'm certain there's nothing under there that will alarm or upset you. It's just, you know, sometimes I'm *sooooo* bored. I need a space of my own. I've sort of claimed the under the bed space as my fiefdom."

"Your … *fiefdom!* You read too much! No, I'm not going to deal with this right now. I can't. I have to sleep. But Robbie, where are Dickens and Yellow Tom? If you don't know where they are, help me find them. If they're under the bed, please get them to come out."

"I believe they're in the closet. I saw Yellow Tom dart in that direction, and much to my shock, Dickens followed. I have never seen him move so fast, ever! But they ran through Evanora's holo, and, I'm sorry Joy, but I became distracted by the scary presence of all those forms of Evanora's holo."

"Yes, Robbie, it must've been extremely disconcerting." I petted him affectionately.

"Extremely," Robbie agreed, milking my sympathy.

"You're so brave, my friend."

He purred audibly.

I stood and went to the closet. I peered around on the floor, but didn't see them. "Dickens, where are you, sweetie? Everything is okay. It's time to go back to bed." I heard a tiny, faint meow, but I couldn't figure out where it came from.

"Yellow Tom? Where are you kitty?" I shoved the clothes around and then saw a cardboard box on the floor in the corner of the closet. I didn't even know what I had in the box. I couldn't remember putting it here. I went up to the box and peered inside. Sure enough, there lay Dickens, with Yellow Tom wrapped around him protectively.

"*Awwww...* How sweet! Yellow Tom, you're adorable, taking care of Dickens like that." I reached in the box, and pulled out Dickens, hugging him tightly. "Everything is all right, my special Dickens-kitty, you're fine." Yellow Tom jumped out after us.

"Let's go to bed!" I went to the bed, kicked off my shoes, put Dickens on the bed, threw back the blankets, and plopped down, then threw the blankets over me. Yellow Tom and Robbie jumped up on the bed and the three cats nested together. "Lights out."

The lights went out.

I was startled awake by a horrible, blaring, blasting, bleating sound.

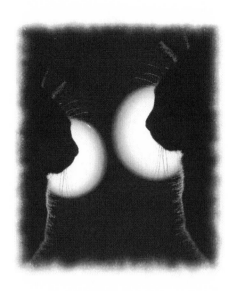

Chapter 17
The Most Peculiar Creatures

"*W*hat?! What?!" I jumped up and looked around, foggy, nearly in a trance state, trying to come out of a deep, deep, sleep.

Bright sunlight came into the room from all the windows. "*Aargh*! Herkimer's Angels, what time is it?"

"The time is nine-thirty-nine, a.m." the modulated feminine clock voice that resided in Robbie said all too calmly.

Robbie stood by the bed, holding out a cup of tea, and two of the special Turkish delight confections Evanora had given me. I pulled myself up to sit. "Where did that horrible sound come from, Robbie?" I asked, gratefully grabbing for the tea. "Did you make tea for me? Is it the tea Evanora gave me?"

"In reverse order, yes, it's the tea Evanora gave you. Yes, I made it. And the horrible sound came from me. You said you needed to sleep three or four hours and it's been almost five. I tried to wake you up gently, but you weren't responding. I had to step it up, several times. Pretty horrible, all right. But I brought you these treats."

I sipped the tea. "*Oh!* So lovely!" I took a deep breath, inhaling the aroma of the tea, as satisfying as the flavor. "*So lovely*, but I don't have time to enjoy it. I'll have just one of the Turkish delights, and save the other for later when I can take my time to savor it, in a relaxing moment. Assuming that I ever get to have such a moment again." I jumped from the bed, eschewing even a shower or changing clothes.

"I've got to find Booji. Are you coming with me today, Robbie?" I let myself have fifteen seconds of pleasure with the Turkish delight, standing there in yesterday's clothes.

"But of course, Joy. I'm as committed to finding Booji now as you are."

"Excellent! Did any communication come in from Travis, or Evanora, or even, heaven forbid, Bruno?"

"No, Joy, no messages from any of them."

"Good! Car, please come by the back door," I said into my wrist comp. "I'll be leaving directly with Robbie."

I flew around putting out bowls of cat food and fresh water for the two kitties who would be home alone, possibly all day.

I grabbed up my backpack, and flying by the mirror, ran my fingers through my short, mussed up hair. "Go back to bed," I told my reflection. If only she could do that and get some good rest while I ran around, it would be so helpful. But science hadn't figured out how to do that yet.

"Let's go!" I ran through the house, leaving Robbie behind me to lock the door. When I turned to see where he was, I was surprised to see that Yellow Tom stood right beside him. "What are you doing, Yellow Tom? You can't come with us."

"Why not, Joy? He might be super helpful, and he seems determined to come along. I'd think that all he's been through, he'd be perfectly happy to stay in the cozy house, in the cozy bed. But apparently, he's as much up for adventure as we are."

I shrugged. Robbie made a point, Yellow Tom might be useful. But I'd have to worry about him every time I opened the car door, to make sure he didn't escape. Not that I thought he'd be inclined to, but that's sort of in a cat's nature, to go through open doors. I didn't have time to mull it over right now.

"Let's go then, everybody on board." Robbie laid down on the front seat next to Yellow Tom. "Robbie, you know you have to get in the car seat. Don't waste my time, please."

"But Yellow Tom doesn't have to."

"If I had another car seat, I'd attempt to put him in it. Conversely, I could put him in the cat carrier, but he'd have to be in the back, and be enclosed, so he wouldn't be much help to us, and he might as well stay home. Do you want him to stay home?"

"No, I want him to come with us. But I want him to ride in the car seat, and let me sit on the seat."

I picked Robbie up, not all that easy as he was pretty heavy, and put him in the car seat, pretty darn well exasperated with him. I locked him in place.

"Not to say that Yellow Tom isn't completely precious, because he is. But, Robbie, if we got in an accident, *heaven forfend!*, you colliding with the windshield would cost me considerably more than if Yellow Tom did. And, quite frankly, he is much more likely not to be harmed with his real cat bios and his many, many cat bones, than if you were to fly into the windshield. Now then, I am *not* going to say it again."

During my soliloquy, I finished locking Robbie in the car seat, scurried around the car and climbed in, latching my own seatbelt. "Let's go, Car. I think we might start out where we left off when we found Yellow Tom, what do you think, Robbie?"

"I agree."

The car took our directive and headed for the location where we'd been when we found Yellow Tom.

"Are you going to talk with Evanora?" Robbie reminded me.

"Oh darn-darn-darn a sock. I forgot. I guess I have to talk with her. I don't want to right now. First of all, I overslept, but I clearly needed it."

"You really did," Robbie said. "Do you want me to share with you some of your bios?"

"Not now, Robbie. I'm sure they're showing I need one thing and another. But right now is not the moment I dare add any more stressors to my very full plate."

"Well then, I'll just tell you, that those five hours of sleep you got were really, really, *really* good for you.

You slept unusually deeply. It was as good for you as any of your rare eight hours of sleep, where you often don't actually sleep very deeply."

"Good to know. More information than that I don't need right now. Call Evanora," I said into my wrist comp.

Immediately, her holo came up. "Oh, Joy, I'm so glad you called. I've been waiting and waiting to hear from you."

"Sorry I'm a bit late, Evanora. Much to my surprise, I fell deep asleep and overslept. So badly needed! But I'm now on the road, looking for Booji. We're near where we found Yellow Tom yesterday, at the edge of the forest. There's quite a bit of traffic, so the car and I have to keep our wits about us."

Heady Honey's, or was it Heady Sweetie's?, face came into the picture.

"Heady hears your voice. She remembers you!"

"Hi, beautiful Heady," I said, happy to see the exotic creature. "Okay, Evanora, we're close to where we're going to start hunting for Booji today. Call me if anything important turns up, but otherwise, it's better if you let us do what you want us to do."

"Us? Is someone with you?"

"Robbie, my robot, and, yes, a beautiful yellow tomcat we found while looking for Booji. A beautiful cat who had been taken out to the forest and abandoned by his people."

"Oh no, how terrible! I would give anything to have my kitty back, while someone *abandons* a beautiful creature. There is no logic."

"Very, very true, Evanora. The human family is made up of the most peculiar creatures. All right now, I'm signing off. Be patient. Be strong. You'll hear from me later. Be sure to let me know if you get any news."

"You'd better believe I will, Joy. I'm just sitting here waiting to hear from anyone, going crazier than usual. I'm so torn! It feels like I should be out looking for Booji and Birdie, while at the same time, I feel I have to stay here, in case either of them returns. And yet, it's almost impossible for me to wait. I'm a doer not a sitter."

"The lessons of patience are often life's most difficult. Picture the two of them home, that's the best energy you have."

"Thank you, Joy, you're absolutely right. Catastrophic pictures only produce catastrophe. Calm pictures produce solutions."

"Lovely," I reassured Evanora. "Just keep...."

The car suddenly slammed on the brakes.

Chapter 18
Little Black Cat

"*Look! Look! Look!*" Robbie yelled, as a little black cat flew across the road in front of us, in a snap-shot second.

"*What?*" Evanora cried.

"Good job, Car! A black cat just darted out in front of the car. It looks like we've found another lost cat. Gotta go, Evanora." I reached over and released Robbie from his confines. "Open passenger door," I ordered while I held on to Yellow Tom, not sure what to do. I didn't want to lose him now, and I needed to get the cat carrier to where I saw Robbie disappear among the ferns.

I held Yellow Tom as I hurried to the back of the car, then told the cat carrier to follow me. I returned to the driver's side door. "Open door," I ordered. I put Yellow Tom on the seat, closed the door, and hurried to the side of the road, with the graphene carrier coming along beside me.

There was a moderate amount of traffic, and a couple cars slowly went around us. "Pull over as far as you can, Car." The car complied. Yellow Tom, standing with his paws against the window, watched me intently. I walked up to where I thought the black cat had scurried into the ferns. "Can you see the little black cat, Robbie," I called softly.

Robbie turned on his holo so I could see what he saw. But all I saw were fern fronds. Robbie crept low to the ground through the ferns. I didn't know how he had any idea where to go, but soon I saw the little black cat crouched down right in front of him.

Robbie stopped, sat, and meowed.

The little black cat turned and looked at him, with, I could have sworn, a quizzical expression. Then, she let out the most delicate, plaintive little meow anyone ever heard. She was afraid, confused, and very, very, cautious.

Robbie did not move, but stayed sitting right where he was, continuing the conversation. His tone was so sweet, I don't think I'd ever heard him sound quite like that. I saw the visible tension in the little cat's muscles relax a bit. Robbie began to purr, and the little black cat came up to him.

Oh! It was so touching! She looked at him as if asking, "can you help me?"

Robbie gently nuzzled her neck, and the little cat relaxed even more. Then he made some soft, reassuring conversation and stood, beginning to move toward me through the ferns. He looked back over his shoulder after a few strides, only to see that she had not moved. He went back to her and offered some more of the cute cat chat, while nudging her.

I was sure he was saying to her in cat, "Come on, I'll make you safe." He wouldn't leave her side until she stood. Finally, she did. He took a step, and she took a step.

"Hooray," I said to myself, hoping the progress would continue. Before long, the ferns parted, and Robbie came out with the little black cat beside him. However, she took one look at me and the cat carrier, and dove back among the ferns.

"It's the cat carrier," Robbie said.

"All right, I'll have it move it to the back of the car where she can't see it."

The graphene carrier moved behind the car upon my direction. I moved a few steps closer to Robbie and the little black cat, then sat down among the ferns. I didn't care what anyone driving by might think of me, but I hoped no one would stop out of concern. Robbie went back into the ferns and soon came out with the little black cat beside him again.

"Hello beautiful Little Black Cat," I said, naming her, slowly moving my hand toward her.

Purring and meowing, Robbie came to me, then looked back at Little Black Cat. She was now only about five feet from me. I petted Robbie to reassure her.

She studied my gestures for a few moments. Robbie went back to her and again encouraged her to come to me.

Finally, she took a few cautious steps toward me. When she was close enough for me to reach her, I petted her. Ah, sweetness! She had the softest fur I'd ever felt. I picked her up, braced for her to scratch and bite, and wishing I'd put on the gloves I brought and cleverly left in the car. But she relaxed in my embrace.

"Poor little black kitty, all alone, out in the forest. How did you come to be here?"

"I think she's the offspring of a feral cat," Robbie said. "She showed me a picture of never having been close to people, only foraging their campsites after they've left."

"Oh my goodness, even more amazing then, that she came up to me. She never would have, had it not been for you, Robbie."

"I'm sure you're right. I think I can say that without sounding vain."

"It's the truth, not vanity." Little Black Cat made a soft growling noise. "I wonder why she's growling now."

Robbie watched her closely while he spoke, "I think it's because I'm speaking human to you."

The little cat growled again. "I think you're right," I agreed. "And who can blame her? It must seem very strange to hear a cat speaking human. Even so, she's pretty darn smart to pick up on it."

"She's exceptionally smart."

I slowly stood and walked to the car. "We've got to get the car off the road. The traffic is increasing." I wanted to put Little Black Cat in the cat carrier for her own safety, but I couldn't tell if she would have it. Plus, it just dawned on me, that perhaps she and Yellow Tom would not get along. Goodness! So many problems!

I spoke in a quiet voice while cuddling her, as I came around to the passenger side back door. "Open!"

I directed. The door opened, and I sat inside with the little cat and closed the door. "Robbie, please bring the cat carrier around to the driver's side back door, and set it on the seat. I'll see if I can back her into the carrier."

I kept her facing me while Robbie put the carrier on the back seat beside us. "Now, little black kitty don't be afraid, this is for your own good and safety." I rapidly backed her into the carrier and closed the door.

"*Yowwwwl*," she cried piteously.

Yellow Tom, who had been standing up against the front seat facing us, jumped into the back and put his nose against the cat carrier door. He meowed sweetly, but he only terrified her more.

"*Yowwwwl, yowwwwwwwl!*" she screeched, taking me beyond my wits end.

Chapter 19
A House and Car Full of Cats

"Oh, dear, Little Black Cat. Yellow Tom is just trying to make you feel better."

Robbie had come around to my door, and I let him in. "Let me see if I can calm her." He moved across the seat to the cat carrier, and Yellow Tom stepped back. At the sight of Robbie, Little Black Cat calmed down.

I shook my head, defeated. "It looks like you get your wish, Robbie. I can't possibly drive with her yowling like that, and we must get off this road, it's too busy to be safe sitting here." I returned to the driver's seat and looked back at Robbie.

Virtually grinning, he sat hunkered down in front of the cat carrier. "I'll be fine, Joy. And look how quiet and happy Little Black Cat is."

"All right." But what am I to do now? I wondered. It seemed like the only practical thing I *could* do would be to go home and drop off Little Black Cat. I needed Robbie to watch for Booji in the front, and I couldn't attend to Little Black Cat and look for Booji at the same time.

"Okay, Car, let's go home," I said.

"No!" Robbie protested from the back seat. "We still have to find Booji!"

"I know. But there's too much going on *in* the car for me to focus on what we're looking for *outside* of the car. I'll drop off Little Black Cat, then we'll resume our search."

"All right then," Robbie said. As if I had to get his approval!

"Hey! Who's the boss here?"

"You are, Joy," Robbie said, chuckling.

"Just so we have that straight!"

"I wouldn't want to be the boss of your life, Joy. It's enough to keep the many plates I'm responsible for, spinning."

"Yes, and thank you! I'm so much more productive with you in my life."

"Good to know," Robbie said in a satisfied tone of voice, then meowed at the little black cat.

I soon pulled into the driveway at home. "You two stay here," I said to Yellow Tom and Robbie as I gently took Little Black Cat out of the carrier and went into the house. I took her to the bedroom and closed the door.

Dickens, in his usual place in the middle of the bed, opened an eye to look at me, wondering what I was doing as I never closed the bedroom door. I took Little Black Cat to the bed and sat down with her.

"Dickens, this little black cat is going to stay with us for a while, and right now, I need to leave you alone with her. Will you be all right with that?" I put her down beside him. He sat up and looked at her. She came up to him and licked his shoulder. He began to purr and lay back down, and Little Black Cat lay down beside him.

"*Ohhhh!* Fabulous!" I poured her a dish of dry cat food and a bowl of water, showed them to her, and set them by the bed. "Here's your very own food and water."

Then I brought the cat box from the bathroom into the bedroom and closed the door to the bathroom, thinking that the fewer places she could go, the better it would be for both of us. "Here's the cat box, which you've probably never seen in your life. Oh please Little Black Cat, please figure out what it's for, and use it if you need it.

"Okay, you two, be good until I get back!"

I left the bedroom, closing the door behind me and hurrying back to the car. "Okay Robbie," I said before even glancing around, ready to have our little argument that he must be in the car seat. But, lo-and-behold, there he sat! In the car seat!

Miracles abound!

"Wow Robbie!"

"I know. I'm amazing."

"Yes, you are, my friend." I engaged the car seat latch and gave him an affectionate pat on the head. "Super-duper amazing, that's my Robbie. I think Little Black Cat will be fine. She went up to Dickens and licked him, and he started purring. So, I guess they'll get along. We can check in on them via the holo."

"Shall I return to where we found the black cat?" the car asked.

"Let's head in that direction." But even as I said it, I felt a strong hesitation. After a couple minutes, a compelling, unabating urge to go in a different direction nagging at me finally won.

"Take a left at the next corner and let's head north for a while."

"Yes, Dr. Forest."

The car turned left at the next corner and we headed north on a road I had never been on.

"What are you thinking, Joy?" Robbie asked.

"I don't know. I just have this … pushing … sense of … *urgency*."

"Is it a psychic pick up?"

"Perhaps. Am I picking up on Booji? Maybe. I'm certainly attracting cats that are *not* the one I'm looking for. I'm simply following my instinct."

What more did I have to go on?

"I have a house and car full of cats, none of them Booji."

"All too true," Robbie agreed. "Lots of cats, none of them Booji."

I pulled up the holo of my bedroom to see how Little Black Cat was doing. She was meowing and climbing the curtain.

Excellent! Yay! Fantastic! Just what I always wanted, a cat who climbed the curtains, I noted to myself in silent sarcasm. At least she was a small cat, maybe the damage wouldn't be horrible. Sighing deeply in resignation, I shut off the holo.

To take my mind to something more pleasant, I decided to replay the few good moments I had with Travis early this morning. Some people might say there wasn't much there to think about, but I don't need much to be entertained.

A small smile grew inside my mind, when Robbie suddenly shouted incoherently at the top of his voice, and Yellow Tom, who had his front feet up against the passenger window watching everything go by, began yowling even louder than Robbie.

The car came to a screeching halt.

Chapter 20
Detective Gorgeous

"What in the name of Jupiter is going on with all of you?!"

Robbie pointed downhill, wordlessly.

I looked to where he pointed and saw a huge path of disrupted weeds and grass and brush and even a couple of mowed down small trees. I thought I saw the glint of metal far below.

"Stay here," I said, grabbing my AR glasses and scrambling out of the car. I peered down the hill and saw that the glint of metal was the back end of a car. It looked like it was on its side.

I put my AR glasses in the car. I didn't need them to get down the hill, and I didn't want to risk damaging them in case I too rolled down the very steep incline. Slipping down the side of the hill, I heard the passenger door open. Looking up, I saw Robbie and Yellow Tom get out of the car.

"Robbie, don't let Yellow Tom out! What are you doing? He'll run away!"

"I told him I'd only let him out if he stayed with me."

"And you think he both understood you and will *obey* you?"

"I do."

The two of them came down the hill together toward me. I continued down the hill. Ten feet further, I saw the roof of a green car on its side, blending so nearly with the foliage that if a person wasn't specifically looking for something, they'd miss it.

The unbelievably steep hill was a terrain of giant loose rocks and a slippery slide of shale—practically impossible to traverse and stay standing. The two cats caught up to me, then ran ahead.

My heart pounded as I tried to stay on my feet on the slippery hillside. My heart also pounded, fearing what I might see. A few more feet, and I saw the entire car, laying on its passenger side. I was relieved to see that it didn't look as though it had rolled, but had simply slid down the steep hill.

I finally slid down to it. As I came up to the car, Yellow Tom jumped up on it and peered down through the driver's side window, now the top surface of the car. He began to cry and to paw at the glass frantically. Robbie jumped up beside him.

"There's a woman in the car," he said. "She looks unconscious, but she's breathing."

Yellow Tom started to try to get through the partially open window.

"Don't, Yellow Tom, don't try to get through that window. You'll hurt yourself!" But the next thing I knew, he'd managed to squeeze himself through the narrow space, much to my amazement. His behavior astonished me, and I wondered if he'd been trained as a rescue cat.

The car was firmly wedged against a tree and sat among a great deal of virtually impenetrable blackberries. I decided against trying to work my way around the front of the car. What if it slipped further? I could become pinned between the car and a tree. But, the other direction around the car was completely overwhelmed with six foot tall blackberries. I thought about jumping up beside Robbie, but could I do that without breaking through a window?

I knew I had to see through the windshield to try to ascertain the woman's condition, and to see if I could get her to regain consciousness. Determined, I started to work my way around the back end of the car and along its side, which tore my clothes and even my skin asunder.

I figured my skin would heal, but the clothes were beyond repair. With a full complement of my favorite expletives, obscenities, and imprecations, I finally made it to a point where I could see through the windshield. There I beheld an unconscious woman, all bunched up against the passenger side door. She wore brightly colored clothes and had a great mass of wild lavender and blue hair. I couldn't help suspecting she was the missing Birdie.

I asked myself why I hadn't dialed 911 or called Travis when I first saw the car. *Weird!* I could only explain it from being in a kind of shock, seeing the car at the bottom of the steep hill. I called 911 on my wrist comp.

"911, what's your emergency?" the automated voice asked.

"Car accident at my coordinates. Injured woman trapped in a vehicle at the bottom of a steep hill."

"Emergency vehicles dispatched," replied the mechanical voice, and clicked off.

I couldn't believe what I was now witnessing. Yellow Tom, meowing in the woman's face, and gently pawing at her while carefully not clawing her. I thought again that he must be a trained rescue cat.

"Travis," I called, "did you hear my 911?"

"I did. I'm on my way."

As I watched the remarkable Yellow Tom diligently attempt to make the woman become conscious, she began to stir.

"Hello!" I called her. "We're trying to help you. Are you all right?"

The woman struggled to regain consciousness, but she couldn't seem to do it. On a long shot, I tried the only thing that came to mind, in the hope my suspicion was correct. "*Hello, Birdie!* Wake up now, Birdie, wake up!"

Now she really started to stir about, struggling to move and to become conscious. But she was in an impossible physical position, all folded up against the passenger door. She had visible scratches and bruises. She tried to mumble something, while Yellow Tom continued to paw at her face.

As her eyes began to open, sirens echoed, sounding as though they were coming from every direction.

Doors slammed on rescue vehicles on the road above. Then Travis arrived in the Space XXX Roadster. He couldn't dare fly down to where I was. I watched as he landed on the road above, behind my car.

Suddenly, a swarm of other cars and people milled about on the road. I had no idea who all was up there.

"Are you Birdie?" I asked. "*Are you Birdie?*"

The woman nodded. Yellow Tom put his paw on her face, as if petting her. Birdie looked at him. "This amazing cat woke me up! Is this your cat?"

"Not exactly," I said. "But he *is* amazing!"

Shale came rolling down the hill around me. I looked up to see rescue workers sliding their way down the hill to the wrecked car, followed by Travis.

Then I saw Bruno up on the road, peering down. *Wow! Even Bruno!* Although Birdie was his case, I could never have imagined he'd get here so fast. But I knew he'd not attempt to come slipping down the shale. He was not built for it—he'd make a roly-poly landslide with his first step.

Other people appeared above, but my attention was drawn away from them by the rescue workers, now at the car, and, of course, Travis, sliding down to the back of the car, an anxious look on his features.

"Are you all right, Joy? Your car's on the road, so I assume you're all right. When I got your call, I thought *you* were in an accident."

"No. But getting around the car to the windshield was as if I'd gotten in an accident!" I held up my bleeding right forearm. "What's important, Travis, is that this is Birdie! And she's talking to me. She appears to not have any serious wounds."

Two of the gorgeous young male rescue workers climbed up on the side of the car and opened the back door. One held the door open, while the other one jumped down into the car. He was now behind Birdie.

"Are you all right?" he asked her.

"Better now, handsome, that you're here!" she crooned, cracking a small smile.

He touched a cut on her face.

"Ouch! That hurts."

"We're going to get you out of here. Are you aware of any significant injuries?"

"No, I don't think so. I'm pretty well banged up, but I don't feel like I have any broken bones."

"We have a harness we can have someone bring down to us to put around you and pull you up out of the car."

"What if you tried lifting me out from above? That might work just fine."

"Let's try it." He looked up at his partner holding the back door open. "We need a third person. Someone to hold the door open, someone to help lift her through the doorway and me down here, helping her get up, and get out."

Travis jumped up on the car. "Let the back door close, and open the front door," he said to the rescue worker holding the door open. "I'll help lift her from up here."

I saw the young man do a double take when he saw Travis. He was impressed. "Yes sir, Detective Rusch!"

With little room to maneuver, they did a sort of dance until the young man had succeeded in opening the front door, after letting the back door down. Once the door was open, Travis leaned down into the car and helped Birdie move about.

"Is this your cat?" Travis asked.

"No," Birdie said. "That woman brought him!" She pointed at me. Travis looked at me through the windshield. "You brought this cat down here?"

"No, He came by himself with Robbie. He's been amazing!"

"*Wow!*" He returned his attention to Birdie. "Are you ready for me to try to pull you up?" Travis asked.

"Sure am, Detective Gorgeous. Not waiting for the light to change."

I chuckled.

"Let's take the cat out first. Joy, are you ready to take him?"

"Absolutely!" I stood from my crouched position while Travis reached down and got Yellow Tom in his hands. He brought him up out of the car and handed him to me. Yellow Tom meowed continuously, keeping his eyes fixed on Birdie.

Next, Travis above, and the rescue worker in the car, worked to help lift Birdie up out of the car. Within moments, she was out of the car and on a stretcher that several other rescue workers had brought down. One of them put a blanket over her, while another took her vital signs.

"I'll have to get into accidents more often," Birdie exclaimed. "I've never had so much attention in my entire life."

She evoked a small chuckle from several of them.

Yellow Tom struggled and struggled in my arms, trying to get loose.

"No, Yellow Tom, you must not get down." Even as I said it, I couldn't imagine how I would hold him and climb back up the shale slippery slide. In fact, I knew there was no way I could. Yellow Tom himself solved the problem. He escaped my grasp, ran over to the stretcher, and laid down on it by Birdie.

"My goodness!" I exclaimed. "Amazing! Yellow Tom is determined that you remain in his care."

"I don't mind! And I hope *you* don't mind my borrowing him. He's remarkably healing."

"I believe he's your cat now, Birdie, if you'll have him. He has no people,—other than you!"

"*Oh! Oh! Oh!*" Birdie cried, hugging Yellow Tom. "I'd *love* to keep him for myself. He is such a beautiful, excellent cat!"

"He is, for sure!" I was almost in tears myself. Sometimes it's simply miraculous the way things work out. Sometimes, there's a large, invisible hand shuffling the details around so that the results work out for everyone.

The rescue workers attached a couple of straps around the stretcher, then looped them onto a hook that suddenly appeared from the sky. The stretcher, with Birdie and Yellow Tom, lifted up into the air.

I watched the stretcher intently, terrified I might see a yellow tomcat flying off of it to the rocky terrain below.

Chapter 21
Who's Going to Take This Cat?

B ut he didn't, and Birdie and kitty landed safely.
"Give me your hands," Travis said. "I'll lift you
up onto the car, so you won't have to work your
way back through all those blackberries. My God, Joy,
you're all scratched up and bleeding. You're in worse
condition than Birdie."

"Yes, I had that same thought." I raised my arms
and Travis deadlifted me up like I was a bag of gro-
ceries. I had no idea he was so strong. Impressive!
Once I was on the car, I looked around for Robbie. He

stood by the car, watching Travis and me intently. We walked across the car and jumped down onto the shale and rocks.

"Come on Robbie," I called to him. "Come over here to us, and let's get back up to the car."

"I can scramble up to the car, no problem," he said. "But it's not going to be so easy for you."

"Don't worry, Robbie," Travis reassured, addressing Robbie for the first time as if he was, well, who he is, an intelligent, thinking, being. "I'll make sure she gets up to the road safely and in one piece. There's quite a lot of activity up there, Robbie, and a lot of strangers. You might be safest to get back into the car."

"Good point, Travis," I said. "The last thing I need on this overwhelming day is for some thief to steal my robot cat while we're busy saving someone. So yes, Robbie, please do get back in the car."

Before starting on the troublesome trek back up the small mountain side, I watched to assure myself that Robbie did as he was bid, relieved to see him climb into the car. "All righty, Travis, I'm ready to tackle this mountain."

"Not quite a mountain, but with this slippery shale, it might as well be."

We slipped and slid. I ended up helping him as much as he helped me. But it wasn't as bad as I expected. This was the payoff for schlepping to the gym three times a week, I told myself. I'd have to remember this occasion on those days when I felt too lazy to work out.

When we got up to the road, we encountered a small crowd.

Evanora was there, hugging Birdie on her stretcher in the emergency vehicle, there was Bruno as I'd already noticed, and there were the parents of Mr. Socks!

"Hello!" I greeted them in surprise. "How is it that you're here?"

"We got a police radio when Mr. Socks was missing," Jennifer said. "By coincidence, we heard the emergency call come up that you were in an accident. We're glad to see it wasn't you in the accident, but that you discovered it. Although it looks like it still took a toll on you," Jennifer said. "My goodness, you're bleeding!"

"Oh, it's nothing really, just a few blackberry scratches."

"That's the worst kind," Jennifer's husband said.

"They were harder on my clothes than me," I laughed with droll humor, pointing at the six-inch rip in my leggings. That's when I saw a notable amount of blood drying. "*Hmmm*, yep, pretty hard on me, too."

There was also an assemblage of lookie-loo strangers. I worked my way through the crowd to get to Birdie and Evanora.

"Oh, Joy, Joy, you found my Birdie!" Evanora moved her hugging Birdie to hugging me. "What would have happened to her if you'd not found her?"

"But, dear Evanora, we don't have to wonder that, now, do we? We have her, and she's not badly injured."

"That's right. We have her now." Evanora returned her hugging to Birdie. "Oh, I just can't believe you've been down there in that car for three or four days … I don't even know how long you've been gone. I've been so upset I've lost track of time. It seems like you've been gone forever.

"Both you and Booji gone. It's been horrible, just horrible. But now here you are, so that's wonderful, but I can't stand the thought of you having been down there night after night. Oh! it breaks my heart."

"Evanora, if you would please let me get a word in edge-wise! Good Lord, this is you all over. Just like the scarecrow in the *Wizard of Oz*. My goodness! I wasn't down there for three or four nights. Or three or four days. I was in a hotel. And then very early this morning, I couldn't stand that hotel anymore. I was out driving around, kind of half asleep because, you know, I need my own bed and I haven't slept.

"I came along here and flew right off the road. *Flew right off the road*, Evanora. Flat out unbelievable. Anyway, I've only been there maybe eight hours. I lost track of time, too. I was pretty darn miserable, I'll say that for sure. It *feels* like I was there for three or four days, or three or four years. Thank goodness for this wonderful, wonderful woman, and thank goodness for this gorgeous yellow cat."

"What a relief! That's fantastic that you were only there today. I mean that's not fantastic, it's terrible but, *ahhhh!* I'm confusing myself!"

"And everyone else in the bargain," Birdie said.

This made them both guffaw loudly, a private joke between them.

"Sorry I destroyed your car, Evanora."

"The car? Oh, pooh, who cares about a car? They're a dime a dozen. Time to get a new one, anyway. Maybe I'll get a Space XXX Roadster, like Travis has. Well, not exactly like his. Not a police car."

They both giggled.

"I'll get a car for folks like us."

"That'd be fun!" Birdie said, grinning.

"We need to take her to the hospital now, to get thoroughly checked over, and make sure there are no internal injuries," one of the gorgeous rescue workers said.

"Yes, Evanora, let me go with these beautiful men!" Birdie said.

"All right, all right!"

"Who's going to take this cat?" the rescue worker asked. "He can't go to the hospital."

"I'll take him," I stepped forward and wrested Yellow Tom from his hold on Birdie. "It'll be all right, Yellow Tom. You'll see Birdie later, when she comes home." I turned to her, "You *are* going back home, aren't you, when you're released from the hospital?"

"Yes, of course."

"And you meant it when you said you wanted this excellent cat for yourself?"

"Oh *YES!* More than I've ever meant anything in my life. That cat and I are destined to be together."

"And so you shall!" I grinned, so happy and relieved for the sweet Yellow Tom.

The rescue vehicle closed up and took off in a show of flashing lights and wailing siren. Sighing a huge, grateful, sigh, I turned to talk with Evanora, when Bruno came up to me. "You found my missing person,

Joy. And just a few hours after I told you about her. You're amazing."

"It was a coincidence."

"I gotta give you a hug for finding my missing person and saving me a ton of work." He grabbed me in his unwanted bear hug, hugging the stuffing out of me, and Yellow Tom, too.

Travis stepped in. "That's enough, Bruno. Good grief, do you really have to be told?"

Bruno reluctantly stepped back a small step. "Yes, I have to be told." He grinned mischievously.

Travis shook his head as if Bruno was a hopeless case, and he could do nothing about it. True, he was a hopeless case, but Travis managed to do plenty about it.

"Let's get back to work, Bruno. There are other lives to save." Travis collared him and they moved off to their vehicles. "Glad you're okay, Joy."

"Me too, Travis. Thanks for helping me up the shale slippery slide."

"Any time!" He turned and gave me his wide, crooked grin that, honestly, could grab any girl's heart. Like the beautiful, violet-eyed Evanora, who stood right by me.

"*Oh my,*" she sighed. "*What a man!*"

"Um-hum," I agreed, holding Yellow Tom close, as we watched the Space XXX Roadster lift off into the blue sky.

Chapter 22
Strange Déjà Vu

After Travis could no longer be seen, I turned my attention to Evanora. "Say, are you all right about having this wonderful cat added to your bestiary? You've seen the nearly mystical attachment he has for Birdie."

"Oh, yes. Of course! He is a most, *most* excellent cat, and more than welcome in my bestiary."

Jennifer and her husband waved as they headed for their car. "Bye," Jennifer said. "I'm so glad you're all right. Mr. Socks sends his love!"

I waved back. "*Awww!* Give him a kiss from me!"

Jennifer chuckled. "Will do!"

I saw the adorable Maisie in the back seat, waving at me, smiling. I grinned and waved back.

Then, suddenly, only Evanora and I, holding Yellow Tom, were standing, alone, in the middle of the road.

"Won't you come over for a cup of tea, dear Joy?" Evanora asked. "I really don't feel like being alone right now. Still worried about Birdie, and, well, I just don't feel like being alone."

Oddly, I felt much the same. After so much excitement, coupled with a *huge* relief finding and saving Birdie, and Travis helping me, and me helping him up the side of the steep hill, and now, they were all gone … I felt oddly lonely. Deflated. I was a balloon and all the air had escaped.

"Of course I'll come over for a wee cup of tea, Evanora."

I followed Evanora to her bestiary, a sight I found warm and welcoming. So different from the first time I saw it! As if a lens had fallen from my eyes and I could see the place as it truly was. Charming, with amazing creatures wandering about, and a little cottage painted different colors. Suddenly, the different colors formed a pattern, and I saw the image it made. I'd not seen the slightest hint of the image on my previous visit.

So mystical and sweet.

I got out of the car, and Robbie and Yellow Tom followed me. Evanora parked her rickety car in a rickety little lean to attached to the house, big enough for two cars. Well, the nicer car presently rested on its side at the bottom of a shale slippery slide, no longer the nicer car.

She came back to me as I stood there with the cats. "Is it all right if I let the kids come with us?"

"Of course, Joy. My goodness, you don't even need to ask. Anyway, aren't you going to leave the beautiful yellow tomcat here?"

"I'm hoping to, and I'm sure Birdie will be glad to see him when she gets home."

"She'll be overjoyed." Evanora moved to the front door. "Come along, everyone."

I spied the Headys. "Oh wait a minute, Evanora. I must say hi to the Headys, if that's all right."

"Again, yes, perfectly fine. More than fine. You must be sure of yourself, dear Joy, and not ask permission for everything."

"I don't want to overstep my welcome." I went to the Headys, accompanied by Robbie and Yellow Tom. The Headys came up to me, making soft little llama sounds. "Hello Heady Sweetie, hello, Heady Honey!" I petted the two of them at the same time between their ears. They made a sound almost like purring.

"Oh!" Robbie said, "they're purring!"

"It sounds like it," I agreed. I looked around the yard and then spied Mr. Quackers. "Hello, Mr. Quackers," I called to him, and was astonished when he came flying across the yard to me. *"Oh, my good-ness!* One does not expect a duck to respond to being talked to."

"Animals are considerably more intelligent than most humans give them credit for," Evanora said. "If you call an animal by name, they know their name, and if they like you, they will come when you call! This is not rocket science."

I laughed. "It's an entirely different sort of science. The science of love, I'd say." I stooped over and petted Mr. Quackers as he quacked up a storm of greetings at my feet.

"Ah, yes!" Evanora declared, "The science of love … the philosophy of love … the emotion of love … and, simply, the love of love."

I nodded in agreement.

"Okay, kids, we'll see you later. Let's go inside, Joy, and Robbie, and beautiful new resident, Yellow Tom."

We passed through the multicolored front door into the larger-inside-than-it-was-outside front room, filled with rich and colorful wingback chairs, tapestries, oriental carpets, and the wonderful wall of books. I'd only been here once, but it felt captivatingly familiar. More than familiar. It felt as though I had been here many times.

"Strange *déjà vu*," I said in a quiet voice.

"Oh, I'm so glad you're experiencing *déjà vu*," Evanora fairly sang.

"At that moment, Rainbow the Peacock came strutting into the room, his tail fully fanned, catching and reflecting the light in the many prisms of his glorious feathers. He welcomed us with his raucous call.

"Hello, Rainbow," I answered. "You're looking particularly enchanting today."

"Wow," Robbie said. "The holos I've seen of peacocks do not do justice to this incredible bird."

"Dear Rainbow is the best of the best!" Evanora said. "Now then, let's take the cats to the playroom. Yellow Tom can begin to get used to his new home, and Robbie might enjoy it, too, if he dares to let his essential cat out!"

Robbie, standing beside me, purred audibly. "Oh, Joy, is it all right if I go to the playroom?"

"It's more than all right. If you'll have fun playing in the cat recreation room with Yellow Tom, I think it's wonderful!" I also thought I'd like to spend some one-on-one time with Evanora, without even Robbie standing by. I could catch him up later if I learned anything important. We went to the back of the house where the bedrooms were, and into the amazing cat playground maze.

"*Oh! My!*" Robbie whispered, standing on his hind legs, and sweeping his front paws out to take in the room. He turned to Evanora. "You built all of this for Booji?"

"I did!" Evanora nodded.

Robbie looked at me, a furrow between his brows.

"Don't get any ideas, Robbie, dear. I neither have a room nor do I have how ever many hours it would take to create such a space. Anyway, if I know you, you'd get bored with it."

"I don't think so," Robbie asserted. He looked around the room again. "But even if I got bored ... if I had such a place of my own ... which I don't, and it seems obvious I'm not going to ... ah, well, never mind, you're probably right, Joy. I'd maybe get bored. But for this moment, I am going to let my essential cat out, and play with the magnificent Yellow Tom, before I never see him again."

"Why, why, *why*," Evanora exclaimed, "would you never see Yellow Tom again?"

"Why would I?"

"You would, because Birdie and I will invite you, and we'll even let Joy come along if she wants to," Evanora chuckled, glancing at me with a wide grin.

"First," I observed, "you get an invitation to have play dates with Mr. Socks, and now play dates with Yellow Tom. Aren't you the lucky kitty?"

"I am!" Robbie swished his tail like he did when he was impatient for something to occur. He looked at me. "Weren't you going to have a cup of tea?"

I laughed and turned to Evanora. "Wasn't I going to have a cup of tea? I believe Robbie wants to begin his play time *right now*."

"You were, and me too! Have fun, you two." We stepped out of the room, and she closed the door. I immediately heard the two cats tearing around the room.

"I hope you have a cat playroom left after they're through with it."

"Not to worry, Joy. It's strongly constructed."

I thought about the little black feral cat in my bedroom with the ever sleeping Dickens. I thought about this wonderful bestiary, and the amazing cat playroom. And the fact that Yellow Tom already cared about Little Black Cat.

"So, Evanora, I have that Little Black Cat that I came upon this morning before saving Birdie." Perhaps it was a tiny bit manipulative to bring up my saving Birdie. But it was for a better cause. "She's feral, born of a feral mother—a little survivor. But she would be so miserable in my small home. And she would be so...."

"Say no more, Joy. I'd love to have her. Can you show me a holo of her?"

"Sure," I said with hesitation, thinking, if I bring up a holo of the little cat shredding the curtains, Evanora will decide this is not the home for her. I produced a holo of my bedroom. Looking around the room, I finally spied Little Black Cat on the bed next to Dickens, sound asleep. I guess the shredding of curtains wore her out. "She's this little curled up ball of black fur next to Dickens, my ever-sleeping cat."

"Oh!" Evanora cried. "She's so sweet! Little Black Cat, you have a forever home here."

Relief! Another weight off my shoulders. "But I have to be truthful, Evanora, she's so exhausted because she's been climbing my curtains." I pulled up a picture of the not quite *entirely* shredded curtain.

Evanora frowned at where I pointed in the holo.

Oh, no ... I thought. *No bestiary for Little Black Cat!*

Chapter 23

Playrooms and Healing Potions

"That? That's nothing! I can get new curtains every day. But a special little kitty who has come to me by this serpentine route only happens due to the movement of great energies. I can't wait for her to be here."

"That makes me *soooo* happy. But more importantly, it will make Little Black Cat happy."

"Good! Now, let us have our tea."

"Yes. Let's." I followed Evanora through a maze of narrow hallways. Where on the planet earth was I? We passed a large oriental carpet rolled up on the floor. I couldn't help asking, "Is that Birdie's?..."

"Yes, yes. That's Birdie's precious carpet. Thank you for your excellent suggestion, Joy. I don't even have to take the carpet to the Himalayas myself to get the carpet rewoven. I found a service that will ship it there and make it as good as new. *Er*, I mean," she tittered, *"as good as old."*

"Yes," I laughed. "As good as old."

"But I haven't sent it off yet, because I'm still considering taking the carpet to the Himalayas myself. It's all dependent on … it's all dependent on…." Evanora began to breathe heavily, and I feared she would start crying.

"I'm profoundly appreciative to the universe for returning Birdie to me, yes. If I can only have one of the two, it would have to be Birdie. But…."

I put my arm around her shoulders. "I know, Evanora. Booji. I know. I understand. I cannot say more than that I empathize. How devastated I would feel if Robbie, or Dickens were … gone." Goodness, I could hardly even say it, as terrible as the merest thought felt.

"The worst part is the guilt," Evanora went on. "One of my affirmations is never to feel guilty, because guilt is the result of giving up one's power to someone or something else. But in this instance, I've earned feeling guilty. Instead of remaining calm, I let drama prevail. The result is I no longer have my precious Booji. And so, I may take the carpet to the Himalayas myself in order to get away from my grief here."

"But, Evanora," I said cautiously, "I know I'm not telling you anything you don't know when I point out that, wherever you go, there you are."

"You're right. I will take my grief with me. But at least I'll have a new experience and be in a different environment." She shrugged. "Anyway, I may not do it, now that Birdie is coming home. She may need me to attend to her cuts and scrapes. And to heal our relationship."

I nodded, remaining silent. Only she could make this decision.

"But!" she snapped out of her melancholy, "Speaking of healing wounds, before we even think of tea, I must, if you don't mind, attend to these wounds you acquired saving Birdie."

"Oh, no, don't bother. They're just scratches."

She pointed to the six inch gouge on my calf. "That's not just a scratch," then she pointed to the long laceration on my right forearm, "and that's not just a scratch. They need attention. They could become infected. If you don't want me to attend to them, kindly please go to urgent care. But they're likely to scar. With my medicine, you will heal fast, and hardly have any scars at all."

I hated the thought of going to urgent care. I much preferred the idea of seeing whatever Evanora may be able to do for my wounds, that I saw now were worse than I had thought they were. And, yes, of course I'd prefer not to have scars. I hadn't even thought about that.

"I'd much rather have you do what you do, if you *can* do something. I didn't realize they were quite as bad as they are. *Adrenaline!* I haven't felt any significant pain. But now that you point it out, yeah, I'm kind of in pain."

"Follow me. You're now about to enter into my inner sanctum, where almost no one else has ever been."

We wandered through three more turns of the maze—well, *I* felt like I was wandering, but I'm sure Evanora was quite purposeful—when we came to a door entirely made of stained glass. Although I felt certain we were in the very bowels of this strange house, a light shined from somewhere, making the stained glass vibrant with translucent colors.

One might think a witch's door to her potions would be composed of mystical and arcane symbols. But this door wasn't. Instead, it was a glorious flower garden, bathed in blue sky and sunshine, filled with a riot of flowers … hollyhock, sweet William, primrose, pansies, iris, gladiolas, and others, receding into the background, so lifelike, it seemed as if I could smell them.

And maybe I did.

I stopped short in awe of the door. "This door is breathtaking."

"Yes. It is," she said simply.

What *was* mystical about the door was the lock. An ancient-looking contrivance of what appeared to be brass and silver and gold. Evanora did something with the lock that I couldn't understand as she didn't have a key, but, somehow, the door swung open. Peering into the little room from the hall, there was no light to explain the light emanating from the stained glass door.

Evanora gestured me to step inside. From the hall it looked like a narrow little pantry. But, like the rest of her house, when I stepped inside, the space expanded into a long, tall, narrow room. All around me were shelves and drawers. I have no idea what might be found secreted away in the drawers, but on the shelves were herbs, hundreds of sorts of plant matter, and mystical concoctions that I had no idea *what* they were.

"Sit on this little stool and roll up your legging, gently, Joy, so it doesn't hurt, while I mix up something to make it heal." I sat on the little stool and folded my legging away from the gouge, wincing audibly as I did so. It was more sore to touch than I could have imagined.

"See what I'm saying? It's worse than you thought."

"You're right." I didn't feel like conversing, fascinated as I was by the space I was in, and in what she was doing, as she pulled one thing and another from the shelves. Putting a jot of this, a tittle of that, and almost a dollop of the other thing into a glass mortar. She began grinding it all together with a glass pestle. The ingredients looked dry, but as she ground them up, they became a paste. *Interesting!*

"We'll let that sit for a few moments while I clean the wounds. This cleansing substance alone will have a significant healing effect." She moistened a towel with it and bathed my two major wounds. I rolled up my other sleeve, where there were multiple small scratches, and then the same with my other leg.

Evanora gently applied the substance, whatever it was, to my poor, broken, skin. It felt wonderfully soothing, and didn't hurt at all.

"That's good. Now the medicine is ready." She brought the concoction she'd made and kneeled on the floor, applying it to my calf. It stung mightily for a moment and then became unbelievably soothing. She wrapped a compress around it, and moved to the wound on my arm, treating it in the same caring fashion. Then she lightly applied what was left of her medicine to the small scratches on my other arm and leg, but didn't bother to wrap them.

"These small scratches will heal rapidly from the medicine. They don't need a compress. But keep the compress on the two larger wounds overnight. You might be surprised how healed it looks in the morning." She fussed about, putting all of her little bottles and vials in place.

"How do you feel?" she asked.

"Good." That's when I noticed I felt a little bit floaty. "I feel a little floaty, Evanora. I'm okay with that, but I don't want to feel a lot floaty."

"You won't. Most people don't feel anything, even right away, let alone after a little while."

She put the finishing touches on replacing everything and closing up the cupboards. "People call me a witch. I don't much care if they do. But they're wrong, of course. I'm a healer. I work with nature, I bring things back into harmony.

"I'm far from perfect! That's obvious with the drama I created with Birdie and Booji. It's all grist for the mill of life. The more important the lesson, the more dramatic."

How true! I thought. Myles came unbidden to mind. *Hmmmm ... but ... what's that lesson?*

Evanora gently pulled my leggings back down over my calves and my jacket over my forearms.

"I feel surprisingly out of pain," I said amazed. "I didn't realize how much pain I was in, until now it has stopped."

"Yes, that is the way of pain for some people. Let's have our tea, shall we?"

"Yes, let's," I agreed enthusiastically, secretly hoping there might be a piece of that amazing Turkish delight in the offing as well, although I didn't say that out loud.

We wended our way around yet more maze-turns and somehow came out in the kitchen. I looked for Mrs. Lark.

Catching my glance, Evanora said, "I gave Mrs. Lark the day off when I went flying from the house to Birdie. I didn't know how long I'd be gone, and I figured she might as well have some downtime."

"Oh," I said, realizing this was another thing Robbie would find interesting. He got whatever downtime he needed in terms of charging up and updating his software but, honestly the thought of giving him downtime, just because he deserved it or might enjoy it, never crossed my mind. "Do you think a robot needs downtime?"

"I don't know about 'need,' it's just a thing I do for Mrs. Lark when I don't have any particular thing for her to do. It saves energy if nothing else."

"That's true."

Evanora opened a cupboard with rows and rows of various sorts of teas. Or I guessed that's what they were.

"Are you going to make me the same wonderful tea you made before?"

"I thought I'd give you a different sort of treat, if you don't mind. It's delicious, but it also has a very soothing healing component."

"Oh! Then, I'm completely up for it. Bring it on." I watched her put together the ingredients with the same intense thoughtfulness that she'd made the healing potion, inclusive of an identical glass pestle and mortar.

I became distracted by movement in the back-yard, and, curious to see what other creatures Evanora had, I stepped out onto the deck. There I observed a *huge* yard, with tall grasses. I saw move-ment among the grass. Curious, I stepped down from the deck, and moved into the grassy terrain. Much of the grass came almost up to my waist. A narrow path had just been laid down by whatever creature had walked by.

I followed the path ... *and then let out a bloody scream!*

Chapter 24

Something Sweet and Delightful

F rozen to the spot, I couldn't move. And I hoped the ocelot I faced would not move, either.

Evanora came running out onto the deck, and seeing what I saw, began screaming too. But, adding shock to shock, she screamed, "*Booji! Booji! Little Boo!*" She ran down off the deck and out through the grasses. Falling to her knees, she wrapped her arms around the ocelot, sobbing. "*Oh, Boo! Oh, little Booji! You came home!*"

Frowning I stood there thinking, thinking, thinking. No ... Evanora had never told me Booji *was an ocelot*. But ... Robbie had said she looked different from usual cats, and the car had mentioned there was something unusual in Booji's DNA.

What an understatement! Why couldn't I exactly see the picture Evanora showed me of Booji? Obvious answer: she cloaked it, thinking that if I knew Booji was an ocelot, I would be disinclined to endanger myself looking for such a creature. But what if we'd found her, and she injured or destroyed Robbie?

However ... Looking at Evanora crumpled on the ground, tears of joy streaming down her face, clutching her precious Booji, how could I be upset with her?

I could not. I was thrilled that Booji had, of her own will, returned home, even if her precious cat was a wild animal.

I could hear Booji purring from where I stood, a good ten feet distant. *Wow!* Quite the motor!

Evanora looked up at me. "Oh, Joy, thank you so much, you found Booji."

"No I didn't! She was just here in your yard!"

"Yes but, if you had not seen her, she may have left again. Now I can apologize to her, and make it up to her, and things will be good again." She looked at Booji. "Things will be good again between us, won't they, dear Booji?"

The cat made sounds that sounded like talking. I didn't know what she said, but she sure had a lot to say.

"Oh Booji! Goodness, goodness! You've had quite the adventure. But are you glad to be home now?"

The ocelot meowed loudly and licked Evanora's hand with her huge tongue. I cringed a little bit, but saw the delight in Evanora's face, and let it go at that.

"You ... you didn't tell me Booji is an *ocelot!*"

"I didn't? *Hmmm*, well, I forgot, I guess. She's just my little Boo."

Inside the kitchen, the tea water started to whistle. It was more like a screech.

"Oh, Joy, could you possibly *please* go in and turn off the tea water? You're such a dear, thank you so much. I need a few more bonding moments with Booj."

"Sure." I returned to the kitchen and went to the contraption making the noise. I'd never seen anything like it. It had a mystifying tangle of pipes attached to the wall and I had no idea how to make it stop screaming. It gave me a headache, and I couldn't continue to stand right by it.

I stepped back out on the deck and called to Evanora. "I can't figure out how to turn the thing off. I've never seen anything like it."

"Oh, sorry, Joy. Of course you wouldn't know how it works. I'm so preoccupied with my darling Booji." She struggled to stand while hanging on to the ocelot. Carrying her like a baby, she came up the steps and into the kitchen, while I kept a goodly distance from them.

Adding surprised to surprise, Evanora placed Booji on a chair. "Now sit right there Booji while I make tea. Do you mind closing the deck door, Joy? Thank you so much."

I was thinking that I pretty much wanted the deck door to remain open, in case I needed to make a rapid retreat. But I did as Evanora asked, putting my fate in the hands of my angels.

"What were you thinking?" Evanora asked.

"I was trying to turn the noise off. But I couldn't figure out how to do it."

"Not you, dear Joy. I'm asking Booji what she was thinking by going off like she did."

"Oh yes, of course." Silly me, to imagine Evanora would be talking to me, when Booji had just returned.

Evanora continued to bustle about making the tea, putting together tea service with honey and oat milk, and, most importantly, placing several of the delightful Turkish delights on a beautiful, hand-painted plate depicting a bucolic forest scene.

Even so, did I really intend to sit across a little kitchen table from an ocelot, sitting on the adjacent chair, while I genteelly sipped tea and noshed on Turkish delight?

Apparently ... I did. Evanora brought the tea tray to the table, poured a cup for me and a cup for herself, then, arranging her teacup and a small dish with a couple pieces of the Turkish delight at the chair where Booji sat, she took the cat up in her arms, and sat. Reaching around Booji, she retrieved her tea cup and took a sip.

I watched in hypnotized fascination.

"Are you not going to drink your tea?" Evanora asked.

"I am." I took a small sip, while not removing my eyes from the truly, remarkably, gorgeous animal. "Booji is an ocelot," I said with the greatest simplicity. "You do know that don't you?"

Evanora laughed. "Of course I know Booji is an ocelot. She's a rescue ocelot. Isn't she beautiful? Isn't she sweet?"

"She's extremely beautiful. I've never been anywhere near an ocelot, and she's gorgeous. But now that she's back, what about Yellow Tom and Little Black Cat? The won't be safe with an ocelot."

"Not true. Booji is wonderful with domestic cats. She's been with me since she was a kitten, and there's always cats around. She loves other kitties. What she does not do well with is her own kind. That is to say, her biological kind. They frighten her terribly because they really are wild, and Booji is not. She's a lover not a fighter. Aren't you my gorgeous baby?" She gave Booji yet another hug, and Booji redoubled her purring, if that was even possible.

"How do you have chickens and ducks with this huge cat?"

"She's strictly vegetarian. In fact, I can't get her to eat anything but her special sweet potato and nutrients food I've made for her since she was a kitten."

"What has she been eating while she's been gone?"

"Good question. What have you been eating since you've been gone, Booji?"

Booji looked at Evanora and started talking. She had a lot to say. Evanora nodded and nodded.

"What an adventure! She says she needed a walkabout. She says she was always going to come home, but she needed to explore. It's probably something in her genetic make up. Anyway, she says she couldn't find her food anywhere. She didn't know that it wasn't out there, readily in the world for her to get. Now she does!

"Now you know what your mom does for you, don't you? I make all of your food the way you like it, and you'd better think twice before you leave home, dear Booj. You were lucky, but there are people who would do you harm."

She returned her attention to me. "Now then, we have a bit of business to attend to, Joy. Please open up that cupboard right there, and you'll see several canisters."

I got up and opened the cupboard she pointed to. Sure enough, there were several canisters neatly lined up.

"That's right. I'd like the canister that has planets on it, yes, that's the one."

I took the canister to Evanora, feeling just slightly more comfortable around Booji, knowing she's always had a domestic life.

"Open it. Whatever is in it is yours."

I opened the canister. It contained a huge bundle of one-hundred-dollar bills.

"There you go, dear. Take that, please with my extreme gratitude."

I counted it. "There's an even fifteen-thousand-three-hundred-dollars here, in cash. Cash, Evanora. Not a common sight."

"Excellent! Fifteen grand, that sounds about right."

"No, not right. I didn't find Booji. All I did was find other cats."

"And a wonderful thing, that! Besides, you did *everything*. And had you not just now seen Booji, she may very well have gone off again. But setting all that aside, Joy, what is of the most supreme importance is that *you found Birdie!* She may have died if you hadn't come along."

There was truth in that. "But I don't expect to be paid for finding Birdie!"

"I believe in karma, sweet, kind, Joy. I have more money than I know what to do with. It just keeps growing! My financial adviser makes it grow. When he calls me, he asks me what I want to do with my money, but I have no idea! I tell him to do with it as he pleases. Of course, he pleases to make it grow as he makes a tidy commission. And so it gives me great pleasure to give you a few bucks. I'm thinking you can use it."

I reflected on Grifter, my horse at my aunt and uncle's farm, who never had a small bill. I thought of the notion of making something like a playroom for Robbie, I thought of the new neural net I desperately needed, as my current one was so full to bursting, it could hardly hold any more of my endless creations.

Yes. I could use the money. I nodded.

"Very well, then. All's well that ends well, is this not true?"

"Truer than true, dear Evanora. Truer than true."

We settled back with our amazing tea in a quiet reverie. I indulged myself three—not two, not one—but *three* pieces of Turkish delight, and watched as lovely pastel colors rose up around Evanora and Booji.

Hmmm, something sweet and calming and delightful in the special tea.

The End

Don't miss any of Joy's mysterious adventures! Here's the first two chapters of
A Gaggle of Geese:

Chapter 1

A Gaggle of Geese

*M*adagascar! Fascinating Madagascar—land of lemurs and baobab trees. I stood in the midst of a virtual baobab forest, looking up at the towering trees, their bare trunks reaching up to their canopy far overhead ... when my computer had the temerity to interrupt.

"Incoming...."

"Hush!" I ordered.

"Designated urgent," my computer dared to continue.

"*From who?*" It had better be pretty darn important.

"From Sophia."

Sophia? What could she possibly have to say to me that was urgent? "Pause program. Connect with Sophia."

"Oh, Joy! I'm so sorry to bother you." Sophia came up in the holo before me, herself among the exotic baobab trees. In her trademark flowing lavender clothing, she was stunning, and the baobab trees appeared to approve her presence and beauty. "I'm sure it's the middle of your workday."

Inwardly, I nodded. "Well, my computer said you designated the call as urgent...."

"Very urgent, Joy, yes it is! You know the goose girl, and, well, the most terrible thing has happened— the most terrible thing! The statue has disappeared. Everybody is in a state. I never saw such a frenzy at her place, as you can imagine...."

I. Had. No. Idea. What. She. Was. Talking. About.

"Dear Sophia, I haven't the foggiest notion what you're talking about!"

There was a *verry* long pause. Then softly Sophia said, in a curious, utterly bemused tone of voice, laced with disbelief, "You ... you ... you don't know who the goose girl is?" Her disbelief knew no bounds.

"I have not the foggiest notion, dearest Sophia, who the goose girl is and, well, *what*," I paused. I restrained myself from adding an expletive of some sort in that pause. *"Statue?* What statue? You've mentioned a statue I know nothing about and tell me that it's missing. Which I also do not know.

"As you can see, I'm completely in the dark." I looked longingly at the faded baobab trees outlining Sophia. Oh, yes. I had the strongest sense that yet another project was about to be seriously interrupted.

Sophia carried on in her vein of disbelief. "I cannot fathom how you can be a self-proclaimed researcher of the human family, and not even know about an important individual in your own, *practically literally,* backyard."

Duly reprimanded, I refused to feel guilty. "Well, sweet Sophia, I imagine that very factor leads to my stunning ignorance. I don't *do* research in my own backyard." I waved to the baobab trees around her that she could not see. "I'm generally retained to do research on cultures in other parts of the world, you see."

"Well, that does not preclude you from being aware of what is in your immediate surroundings."

Hmmm... what was in my immediate surroundings were the baobab trees of Madagascar. But it wouldn't serve to point that out. What *might* serve in the moment was to try to figure out why the holo of

Sophia hovered in my paused project. "I'm unclear, dear Sophia, why you're calling me."

"Isn't it obvious? We need you to discover who stole The Goose Girl Statue."

"I'm confused. Is there a goose girl, or a Goose Girl Statue?"

"There's a goose girl, and there is a Goose Girl Statue. You're needed, Joy. You're very much needed *here*. Please come! People need their healing."

First of all, Sophia needs me to look for a statue, which is *not* on my job description, and now she's asking me to heal people.

"I'm sorry, Sophia. I haven't been known for healing people."

"Oh my goodness!" Sophia sighed with obvious exasperation. "Of course you don't heal, no one's asking you to heal them! Again, we need you to look for The Goose Girl Statue. The Goose Girl Statue is what heals." Sophia now talked very slowly, like talking to a somewhat slow child. In which case, I wondered why she felt I was up to her assignment at all, if I seemed a bit slow.

In any case, we had gotten to the bottom of it, and I finally understood why she called. "Oh! I get it now, finally. Sorry for my obtuseness, I really did have my head in the midst of my work. But I think I'm on the same page with you now. I honestly don't imagine I can be of much assistance." But now the problem was, I was intrigued. And even though I doubted I could be of much assistance, I decided to see what all the hoopla was about.

Who was this goose girl that I had never heard of, that apparently everybody else knew?

And! *What* was this Goose Girl Statue that had the purported ability to heal?

Suddenly, this whole mystery was more intriguing than the beautiful baobab trees. "I'll come and see the situation, but to be truthful, I very much doubt that I will be of any assistance. And I'm sure you've called the police."

"No, Joy. I called you first, of course! But if you insist, I'll call the constabulary."

"It's not for me to insist. It seems much more the purview of the goose girl. The living goose girl. Not the statue goose girl. If that makes sense. Which I'm not sure that it does."

"Anyway! Where are you?"

"Ten-eighty-six, north two-hundred-and second street."

As she said it, the location came up on my holo, covering both her face and my ever receding baobab trees.

"That's a..." I started to say as Sophia clicked off. "Church!" I exclaimed.

Chapter 2

The Goose Girl Statue

Sighing in resignation, I got up and started to thrash about under the desk for my shoes.

"Are you looking for your shoes?" Robbie, my robot cat, asked. He'd been sitting by my chair curled up, almost like a bio cat, not only listening, but also recording every word that had just transpired.

"Yeah, I kicked them off, I think, here somewhere."

"No, Joy. They're at the back door."

"All righty then." I reached across the bed and petted my actual bio cat, Dickens. He opened a sleepy eye, almost purred, and went back to sleep. Robbie followed me into the kitchen, on my way to grab up my backpack and put on my shoes. "Car, come to the back door," I said into my wrist comp. I heard it pulling out of the garage.

"Okay, Robbie, I'll be back ... well, I don't know when. Pretty soon I imagine. I don't think this is anything that justifies my precious time, but it'll be nice to see Sophia."

"Can I come along?" Robbie begged. "Please let me come with you."

"No Robbie, I don't plan on being gone very long."

"I never get to go anywhere," he complained.

"That's because your job is to take care of the home. Anyway, that's not objectively true, is it?" I wasn't about to go into the various adventures we've been on outside of the home, that, in point of fact, I'd found it helpful to have him with me on occasion. He is, after all, my supplemental mind!

Backpack over my shoulder, shoes on my feet, I stepped out the door and into the car. "Ten-eighty-six, north two-hundred-and second," I told the car.

"Church?" Cat queried. "On a Tuesday morning?"

"So it would seem. Sophia just called me and said I needed to come because some statue is missing, and, well, this is the address she gave me."

"Oh!" Car said in a surprised voice. "The Goose Girl Statue!"

My car knew more than I. "You know about the Goose Girl Statue? How … why… oh, I'm completely mystified."

"Pretty common information, Joy. I'm surprised you don't know about The Goose Girl Statue. It's practically in our back...."

"Don't say it! So, Mr. Smarty Car, do you know that The Goose Girl Statue is missing?"

"Oh no, that's very bad for the local folks."

"How so?"

"Because The Goose Girl Statue is known to heal pretty much anything that ails a human. Really, how do you not know...."

"Do not say it! I heard it from the lovely Miss Sophia, and I sure as holy-hecky-doo-rue, do not need to hear it from my car.

"Yes, Dr. Forest. As you say. Well, I hope you'll be able to discover the whereabouts of The Goose Girl Statue."

"*Hmmmm*, I doubt that I'll become engaged in that activity. My deadline for the Madagascar project looms. I must not be distracted. I'm going now out of a selfish bit of curiosity, and I thought it'd be nice to see Sophia. In other words, I'm just taking a short break."

"Oh. Yes." The car had a tone of voice. He might as well have said, "We'll see about that."

"I'll not have that attitude from *you*, automobile. You're to drive, not to editorialize."

"I see."

Did I actually hear a very small chuckle, or was it just an engine noise?

No time to contemplate that as we approached a church nestled on the hillside with what appeared to be several hundred people milling about in the yard in the bright sunny day. It had the air of a country fair. Or a revival. Women in colorful, flowing garments stood in bevys like a flower garden gone wild. A few men dotted the landscape. Light sparkled off the church's stained glass windows. With hardly a place to park, my car pulled onto a bit of grass and stopped.

As I began to open the door, a gigantic gaggle of geese came flying and honking, their wings fully extended, directly toward me from across the yard. Was I about to be attacked? I closed the car door and watched the geese as they gathered around my car door, honking and flapping their gigantic and elegant wings.

Why their undivided attention to me, I could not comprehend. I heard my name being called. *"Joy! Joy! Come along!"*

I looked in the direction of the crowd, trying to see who was calling my name, and then saw Sophia coming toward me.

I opened the door a crack. "The geese! They look like they're going to attack!"

She giggled melodically. "No, no, dear. They're a welcoming committee. They welcome everyone. They're happy to see you."

Cautiously, I opened the door and slipped out. The goose conversation augmented in volume. But they did not attack. They gathered even nearer around me, honking, and chatting, and flapping, and, indeed, they seemed as though they could not be happier to see me.

What amazing creatures! They flaunted their wings, extending them full length, their wingspans as much as eight feet across! I made my way among their massive bird bodies toward Sophia as she made her way to me, as the great goose gaggle welcoming committee continued their chorus at the tops of their voices.

So much commotion! Geese, and dozens of women in soft spring fabrics, with a few men looking on, self-satisfied, as if they'd invented the day.

As I tried to take it all in, a loud, reverberating sound shaking the rafters overhead, demanded every-one's attention.

To read more of **A Gaggle of Geese**, or to check out my other books, visit:

www.BlytheAyne.com

You'll also find my books at your favorite book-store.

About the Author....

T hank you for reading *A Clowder of Cats*. Be sure to read all of Joy Forest's mysterious adventures, which take place in the world of the near future.

Here's a bit about me, if you're curious. I live near where Joy lives, but I'm in the present, about ten years before where Joy's story begins. Unless you're reading this ten years from now, and then, well, I'm in the past, and you're in Joy's present.

I live in the midst (and often the mist) of ten acres of forest, with domestic and wild creatures as family and companions. Here I create an ever-growing inventory of fiction and nonfiction books, short stories, illustrated kid's books, vast amounts of poetry, and the occasional article. I've also begun audio recording my books, which, having a background in performance, I find quite enjoyable.

I throw a bit of wood carving in when I need a change of pace. And I'm frequently on a ladder, cleaning my gutters. There's something spectacular about being on a ladder—the vista opens up all around, and one feels rather like a bird or a squirrel, perched on a metal branch.

After I received my Doctorate from the University of California at Irvine in the School of Social Sciences, (majoring in psychology and ethnography—surprisingly similar to Joy's scholarly background), I moved to the Pacific Northwest to write and to have a modest private psychotherapy practice in a small town not much bigger than a village.

Finally, I decided it was time to put my full focus on my writing, where, through the world-shrinking internet, I could "meet" greater numbers of people. *Where I could meet you!*

All the creatures in my forest and I are glad you "stopped by." If you enjoyed *A Clowder of Cats*, I hope you'll share the book with others. If you want to write to me, I'd love to hear from you.

Here's my email:

Blythe@BlytheAyne.com

And here's my website, and my *Boutique of Books*:

www.BlytheAyne.com

https://shop.BlytheAyne.com

I hope to "see" you again!

Made in the USA
Las Vegas, NV
14 March 2023

69055813R00122